G R JORDAN

The Small Ferry

A Highland and Islands Detective Thriller

First edition

ISBN: 978-1-912153-63-3

This book was professionally typeset on Reedsy.
Find out more at reedsy.com

'The axe forgets but the tree remembers'
African Proverb

Contents

Foreword

This story is set across the varying landscapes of Scotland's highlands and islands.. Although set amongst known towns and lochs, note that all persons and specific places are fictional and not to be confused with actual buildings and structures that exist and which have been used as an inspirational canvas on which to tell a completely fictional story.

Chapter 1

The day was just miserable. Grey clouds hung overhead like a never-ending duvet and drizzle fell relentlessly, giving the firth a misty feel. Even the slipway had been damp and bleak, in contrast to just a day ago when everything had been bright and dry. It was not cold but simply dreich, and thankfully the haar, that sea-borne mist that often affected the Scottish firths, was not around.

The ferry was now approaching the landing on the Nigg side of the Cromarty Firth, having left Cromarty less than a quarter of an hour ago. There had not been any chance dolphin sightings, as happened occasionally, and in every way, this had been the most mundane of runs. Even squeezing the third car onto the deck had been dull. There was no desperate movement of other cars to avoid a scrape and the driver had steered the car almost to perfection. Everyone had proceeded inside and stayed out of the drizzle.

His captain was now piloting the vessel in close and Peter stood ready to assist with the temporary berthing at the slipway. The ferry was not one of the RO-RO variety, roll on, roll off, where the cars drove only forward when they manoeuvred. Instead, the cars had reversed on at Cromarty and would now quickly drive off.

Peter was only twenty-one and this had been his first season on the ferry. Although it was May, the season had not taken off due to the recent bout of cold weather and the atrocious snow storms that still nipped into April. *Global warming,* they had said and Peter believed it to be true. But he was careful with his recycling and even walked to his work every day, so his conscience was clear.

With the vessel now berthed at the slipway, Peter operated the ramp and set it upon the concrete, before turning around and waving the cars off the vessel. The first car, a compact red hatchback, drove off quickly without giving a wave. There seemed to be a group of men inside and Peter dismissed them quickly, turning his eyes to the second car, a black and white Mini with two women in the front.

The driver wore large, round sunglasses and had applied some deep rouge to her cheeks. With the exuberant use of mascara, she looked painted, not real, but something from a cartoon or magazine. Red painted nails appeared over the steering wheel and the car jumped forward before it suddenly stalled. The engine was turned over to no avail and then someone exited from the far side.

Peter's eyes were drawn to the blonde hair that bobbed along in a ponytail. A young woman walked to the rear of the car and began to push. He hadn't seen her face but there was little enough action on the ferry, so Peter walked quickly to the rear of the car to assist.

On his arrival, the woman smiled and he guessed she was around his age. She had a pleasant face and looked very trim in her dungarees. There was a flower pin button on them and she had a neck scarf tied around her. Maybe she was foreign. But wherever she was from, she was the most interesting passenger he had seen in the last week.

Someone else exited the car, but Peter only saw the person pass him in the corner of his eye. Together with the blonde girl, he pushed the car off the ferry and onto the slipway. Once they hit the upward slope, the Mini became much heavier and Peter tried to smile nonchalantly while his muscles strained at the weight. But he had no effect and was glad when the engine suddenly kicked into life.

And then his heart sank. She would be leaving. As someone passed behind his blonde-haired passenger, he could only gaze at her for one last look. It was not love at first sight. Rather he was young, and drawn toward this cute girl. She smiled at him and thanked him before stepping forward and kissing him on the cheek. And with that she was back in the car and driving away.

Peter stood watching the Mini disappear before a voice shouted at him. There were cars waiting on the Cromarty side and the third vehicle was still on deck. Sighing and still dreaming of the face of that girl, Peter walked over to the modern Jeep sitting close to the cabin of the ferry.

Something was wrong. The driver was sitting in his seat but the body was slumped forward and the head was on the wheel. Peter opened the door with urgency and tapped the figure on the shoulder. It was a man, older than himself, maybe in his forties, but most definitely not responding. Peter grabbed his shoulders and shook the man hard but his head only swung to the side and Peter saw the eyelids were closed. Peter's hand slid down the man's back as he tried to stop him from falling out of the car seat but then he felt something wet. Stepping back in horror, Peter watched the man fall from the seat and hang out of his Jeep, the legs trapped under the steering column. From this angle, Peter could see the blood on the shirt, staining it a deep red.

'What's keeping you down there?' shouted his captain.

'He's dead, Angus. The man's dead.'

Peter looked down at his left hand which was covered in blood. For a moment, he simply stared at the dark liquid before screaming with such a ferocity that his captain was shaken to the core. Then Peter looked up, saw the ramp and the slipway and ran. He didn't know where he was going. But he was going as fast as he could away from the man before him. All thoughts of the blonde-haired girl were now gone from his mind.

His captain cried after Peter as he ran up the slipway, hand before him, shocking the awaiting cars with his bloody hand. For a moment the captain wondered if he should follow his crewman but he also looked at the body before him, hanging out of the Jeep. He pulled his mobile from his pocket and dialled the same number three times. The phone shook as he put it to his ear and answered the operator's request.

'Police! No, Coastguard. No, ambulance. Just get me someone—there's a dead man here!'

Chapter 2

Macleod looked at the large stones surrounded by the heather that bore a stunning purple. It had been a reasonable climb up the mountain but now at the top of Fyrish, he understood why visitors came up here. He looked out towards Inverness and then round to Alness beneath him. The Black Isle looked stunning and he traced the Cromarty Firth out towards the twin Sutors where it joined the Moray Firth.

'I told you it would look amazing.'

Macleod turned around and opened his arms for Jane to flop into them. She had fought hard up the hill to not give in to her dodgy ankle but she looked exhausted. She was clinging on to him for support and he started to drag her towards a clear patch of heather where they could sit down. On his back was a rucksack complete with a bottle of Prosecco and his fizzy apple drink and they opened up the small lunch they had brought with them.

'You're quite fit, Seoras. I don't know if I can keep up with you.'

'A little less Prosecco, maybe?'

Jane laughed at his tease. Because he was a teetotaller, Macleod made a point of saying that everything bad came from alcohol. He did not mean it, but it was a constant source of jesting.

'It doesn't stop you giving it to me in the evening when you have that look about you.' Macleod shook his shoulders innocently. 'Don't give me that, Seoras. It's fine to give Jane an extra big tipple when Seoras wants to get close. I know you, sunshine, and don't forget it.'

The laughter petered out and Jane became quite serious. 'You are sure you want to move up here? I mean it's a big move, not easy to go back.'

'Do you want to come up?' asked Seoras, quietly, almost scared to push the question.

'With mother passing on, it's changed things, Seoras. I want my time in the sun, I want to really live this latter part of my life. And I think I want to live it with you. So yes, I'm in, Macleod. I'll come up here as soon as you want. In fact, let's go house hunting while we're here.'

'Somewhere for Mr and Mrs Mac—'

'Stop right there, Seoras. I ain't marrying you. I was married before and frankly it was awful. It was like he owned me. Or thought he did. I don't want a ring, no big church wedding, not even a registry office.' Jane turned her back from Macleod. 'If you want me then you take me as I am. I'm sorry if that isn't fitting in with our church life and your beliefs but that's where I am.'

Macleod stared at the long hair flowing from the back of Jane's head. He reached forward and stroked it, then began to caress her neck. As he went to speak, his mobile started a ring tone. Jane had helped him set up several tones and this one was Hope's tune, but only when she rang from the work mobile.

'Get it,' said Jane. 'It'll be important.'

Macleod took the mobile out and worked the passcode. 'Hope, what's the problem?'

Jane now turned around and watched Macleod's face. Macleod nodded as information was fed to him and then he shook his head despite Hope's inability to see his action.

'I'll see you up here. I should be in Cromarty in about three hours. I take it Ross is on the case. No—Allinson, the Stornoway guy. Well, yeah, they do all move about. Okay, let's get moving.'

Jane watched Macleod put away his mobile and then start packing up the lunch. 'Work calls, Seoras? We stayed in Cromarty before, didn't we?'

'Yes,' said Macleod, flatly.

'Look, it was all a bit heavy before the call, so don't think about that now; you need to work. We'll talk later.'

'No, we won't.' Macleod zipped up the rucksack and took Jane's hand lifting her to her feet.

'We need to talk about it, Seoras. I think we need to know where we are going. I'm sorry, but I can't marry. I just can't. It's not a reflection on you. It's me and I—'

'Jane,' said Macleod firmly, 'shut up. We need to get down off this mountain. There's things to do.'

'Don't hide behind the job. You said three hours, you could be there in two, maybe less. Don't stall me—'

'Jane, shut up. We need to get you a hire car.'

'What?'

'A hire car. I'm going to be busy so we get you a hire car and you can find some houses you like. I'll get to see them as and when.' He looked up at Jane and saw a livid face.

'I ain't buying my own house for you to drop in whenever. I

want one to share. Permanently! Did you miss that, detective?'

'Can we go?' asked Macleod. 'We go down and get you a hire car. You find some houses. We go and decide which one we want and then we move from Glasgow to here. No wedding, no big announcement, no fuss. Just you and me and a bottle of Prosecco because after all that I will want to get close. Is that okay? Can we go?'

Jane ran at him and jumped, throwing her arms around him. Macleod rocked and then fell backwards. As he felt the pain run up his back, he also felt a number of wet kisses to his face. 'You gorgeous man, you bloody, gorgeous man.'

'Jane, my back. Woman, my blooming back.'

As Macleod drove the winding road through Jemimaville towards Cromarty, he could still feel where his back had landed on a stone when Jane had jumped on top of him. He squirmed in his seat, trying to somehow caress it. However, he was smiling like a crazy person. There had been no long debate, no weighing up of the pros and cons, he had just gone with his feelings. His former wife would have been astounded but she would also have approved. Jane had that effect on him, making him more impulsive. And right now, it felt good.

From the road, drizzle now falling and the clouds starting to block out the sun, he could see the Nigg yard where vessels and other marine shipping was often unloaded and worked on. In the Firth were a long line of rigs, some with large accommodation blocks, some serious drilling rigs and others which were now simply four legs sticking out of the water. The offshore industry was not in the heyday it had enjoyed before.

As Macleod drove the promenade along the front of the town, he could see a crowd had gathered and was being kept back, held at the small harbour. On reaching it, he flashed his credentials and drove a short distance before parking the car and walking to where the ferry departed the town. When he had been in Cromarty investigating a previous case, the ferry had not been running but now that the tourist season was here, it would depart from the empty slipway Macleod had seen previously.

As he approached the top of the slipway area, Macleod could see the small ferry on the far side of the Firth at Nigg with a large tent covering its deck. But here on the Cromarty side, a man was walking towards him and he extended a hand.

'Allinson, good to see you. McGrath said it was you. What do you have for me?'

'Not a lot so far, sir. As you can see, the ferry is on the far side and I have forensics all over it. Under the canopy on the deck is a Jeep, one of three vehicles to travel across from the Cromarty side. According to the deckhand, three cars got on, including one car of men, another with two women in the front and this Jeep. Everyone went inside because of the drizzle on the crossing and then as they came back in, they returned to their cars. The first car load of men departed. The second car, a Mini, seemed to stall and the deckhand assisted a young woman in pushing it off the deck. He believes someone else got out of the car but he cannot proffer any details about that person.

'Once they got the Mini turned over, it drove off and he checked the third vehicle, the Jeep, when it didn't start. He opened the door and a man falls half out, dead. We're working on some IDs and are trying to get registration numbers for the cars. Right now, I don't have a lot else. It's about a forty-minute drive around the Firth if you want to see the ferry, sir. Although, I'm also trying to secure a small boat to assist us.

'Good, Allinson—bases covered so far. Are you using the hall again that we had last time?'

The officer looked strangely at Macleod before catching on to what he was saying. 'It was DC Ross last time, I believe, but other than that I'm not au fait with the details of the case. But we're using the town hall here at Cromarty. I set up some interview spaces as well as canvassing the local area.'

'Has McGrath checked in recently?' asked Macleod.

'She's about an hour out, sir.'

'Right; do we have anyone who saw the vehicles on this side?'

'Yes,' said Allinson, 'the coffee shop just beside the pier was open and there was a young woman, Gina Walker. She's still there although the shop is closed. The owner has arrived too, a Mr Bean, funnily enough, hence the Bean Shakers Coffee Shack. The girl saw most goings-on but she's been quite hesitant.'

'Okay, I'll go there while McGrath arrives and then we'll take whatever boat you can scramble over to the ferry, Allinson. Good to work with you again.'

Allinson nodded and then turned away back to his team of uniformed officers who were canvassing the area. Macleod had a trust in the man, and knew he would get things set up and running. Macleod preferred to see himself as operating on a higher level, sifting out the real tale of what happened and not having to deal with the minor points of operations. He'd done enough of that in his younger days.

Macleod approached the small coffee house that lay beside the slipway. It was located right at the top and had a number of impromptu tables and chairs made from old wooden structures and barrels. No doubt, on a sunny day it would be a refreshing sight but in the drizzle of the present, he just wanted to go inside.

Opening the door, he realised how cosy a space there was beyond. Jane would have adored it, a real wood burner to sit beside, casual sofa but all quite close together. No doubt a place where people would talk.

'We're closed,' said a voice. It was friendly enough but also abrupt, the voice of a shop keeper.

'Mr Bean?' asked Macleod.

'Yes, but as I said, we are closed.'

'Good, we won't be disturbed. I'm DI Macleod and the man running the investigation into the incident on the ferry. I'm looking for Gina Walker.'

'Of course, won't you take a seat? Gina's just visiting the bathroom at the end there. I'm sure she'll be right along. Can I get you something? A latte perhaps, flat white, cappuccino, or tea?' The man was standing behind a large machine that baristas use and smiling as if he was ready to do his life's calling.

'Thank you, Mr Bean, I'll take a black coffee, please.'

The toilet flushed behind a blue door at the end of the small cafe and a minute later a young woman exited and stopped in her tracks looking at Macleod. Macleod guessed she was not even twenty and seemed to be very nervous. She wore a simple blue jumper and jeans and had a ring through her nose.

'Who's this?' she asked.

'That's the man in charge of the investigation, Gina, a DI . . .?'

'Macleod, Gina. I'm DI Macleod. You look a little on edge, if I may say so. Try and relax, you're not on trial here, not a

11

suspect, just a chance witness. All I want to do is ask a few questions and see what you can recall about what happened. Is that okay?'

She nodded but Macleod didn't feel like she was being truthful. She looked petrified and he wished McGrath was here. She was better with the younger generation.

'What time did you start work today, Gina?' asked Macleod, waving his hand to indicate that the woman should take a seat.

'Just before eight. We open at eight, you see.'

'And do you remember the last run the ferry took today? Do you remember or did you meet anyone who had been waiting?'

'I think so; you see I was serving so I didn't really see them that well and there was a group of men who sat outside. They sent one person in but they were outside. In fact, they were here for a while.'

'Okay,' said Macleod. 'How many of them?'

'Three. But I only really saw the man who came in to get their coffees. He came in twice. Ordered the same thing both times. One latte, a peppermint tea, and a flat white.'

As if on cue, Macleod's coffee was placed before him by Gerrard Bean and the owner sat down behind his employee. The man rubbed the shoulder of Gina Walker in a fashion that Macleod read as close friend, before smiling to indicate things were all right.

'And the man who came in—what did he look like?'

'He was shorter than you, stocky, well-built though. He had a moustache, quite bushy but not so much it looked stupid. He was very polite and paid in cash both times. Was wearing a green coat and jeans. Black boots.'

'You said he spoke politely,' said Macleod. 'Did he have an accent?'

'I think he was English. Sounded very proper. Gerrard will sometimes have Radio 4 on in here when no one is about and he sounded like they do, very proper.'

'Good,' said Macleod, 'Did you see anyone else?'

'There were a few locals in, Annie, George, and the other dog walkers.'

'Excellent, I'll need the names of them all, although, have you done that already?' The girl nodded. Allinson was thorough. 'Did you see anyone in the Jeep or the Mini that got on board?'

'The Jeep arrived and got on without stopping. In fact, the slipway was clear when it arrived and it went straight to the front of the queue. The Mini then arrived and parked behind it. But there was another car that arrived and the three men had a bit of a debate with the last car. I think they wanted on the ferry which seemed strange as they had been here for two rounds of coffee.'

'How agitated were they to get on board?' asked Macleod.

'Very. I could not hear from in here but it sounded very heated.'

'And that was the last you saw of them?'

'Yes.'

'Did you see the licence plate number of any of the cars?'

'No,' replied the woman. 'Sorry, I wasn't looking for that; I was serving coffee.'

'Don't worry, you've been most helpful. Stay here and I will get my officer to come and take you round to the hall we are based in and put you in front of a sketch artist—see if we can't get a better picture of that man.'

The woman nodded, got up, and made her way behind the serving bar. Macleod heard the tap of coffee being emptied and then a fresh load being clicked into the machine.

'Sorry, Sergeant, I didn't ask if you wanted another.'

'Detective Inspector Macleod, but it's fine, I need to get on. You've been very helpful.'

The woman smiled and Macleod congratulated himself on successfully negotiating the one type of witness he was prone to offend with his ways. She seemed calmer now but something was bothering her. It could just be the murder as that was disturbing enough to many people.

'Mr Bean, I'll send my officer to you too. We'll need the names, addresses of everyone that came in here, locals included, and I want to see who made transactions on your till. I don't see any cameras in here; I take it you have no security.'

'Sorry, not yet; we will be upgrading the place soon. But I'll certainly get you what you need.'

Macleod nodded his thanks and left the small cafe and returned to the drizzle outside. He walked across to the edge of the water and stood looking at the ferry, berthed at the other side of the Firth.

Alive when you departed, dead on arrival. At least the suspects are narrow. Killed on a ferry, but who and why? I need names and registrations of vehicles.

Chapter 3

Macleod was standing at the top of the Cromarty slipway when he heard a shout. Allinson was the owner of the voice and Macleod swore there was a touch more excitement than was professionally required in this situation. A car had pulled up and he recognised the woman climbing out of the vehicle. Watching the rather excited Allinson walk briskly over and shake hands with the woman, Macleod laughed inwardly. He remembered being on the Lewis during his first case with DC Hope McGrath and how she had caught Allinson's eye, and his own if he was honest. Since then, she'd become a close colleague and he'd come to recognise the strong, resilient detective she was.

'McGrath,' shouted Macleod, 'the boat's about to take me over to the ferry. Join me!'

There was a quick exchange between Allinson and Hope, before she hurried over to Macleod. She looked jaded, possibly from the journey, but as ever, she had a warm face.

'Afternoon, sir. Roads were a bit busier than last time we were up here. I got a brief on the way up but it's a bit of a strange one.'

'Indeed,' said Macleod. 'I've had a word with the coffee house owner and his employee, Gina Walker, who is now round at the town's hall, our temporary base, working with a sketch artist. She saw one of the passengers up close. We're running the payment cards too, but I don't think any of our passengers actually used a card at the coffee house.'

'Have you seen the ferry yet?'

'No, the boat's just coming to take us across. Forensics have been all over it anyway, so no doubt I will be chased off.' He grinned at Hope who gave a weak smile back. 'You okay? You seem a little jaded.'

'It's nothing. Bit of boy trouble. Spent most of last night splitting up with someone.'

'Really? I didn't even realise you were seeing anyone.'

'Not all of us are living in Happyland at the moment, sir.'

Macleod went to enquire further but then thought better of it. Over the past months and cases, he thought they had developed a good working relationship but also a friendship beyond the job. Maybe he thought that was deeper than Hope did. But this would not get the case solved.

'Sorry to hear that, Hope. Let's grab the boat and focus on the case.' This produced a smile from his partner and together they walked along to the harbour and boarded a small vessel for the far side of the Firth. The day was still overcast but the visibility meant they could see the entire length of the Firth, from Invergordon right up to Cromarty and then out to the Sutors at the entrance to the Moray Firth.

Admiring the Sutors that stood either side of the Firth's exit, Macleod thought about ferrymen who made this journey back and forth each day. There was such beauty afforded to them, despite the working yard and the rigs set in the Firth behind him. It seemed to him that the Highlands had a way of blending their industry into the landscape so that it became a part of it, rather than an eyesore. Maybe the locals thought different, but he found it to be very different to Glasgow, parts of which he thought could have been better planned. But up here was space and open air. Maybe he was just getting old and mulling over things too much.

'I heard it was one of the smallest ferries still working,' said Hope.

Macleod turned around and saw his partner staring off down the Firth in the opposite direction. 'I think you're right, McGrath,' said Macleod, conscious that there were people within earshot. He only ever used her first name when they were alone or out of work. 'It seems three cars is its maximum. There seemed to be a desperate push by a car load of men to get on the ferry. So you have a single driver in the Jeep, blocked in as he has to either reverse on or off the ferry. In front of him, and embarked second, is a car of female passengers, three, we think, though the deckhand only clocked two. And then this car of men, that raced on last. But they had been at the coffee house for ages.'

'Somewhat too keen,' said Hope. 'And then getting off the ferry, there was a breakdown with the female car. Someone gets out and then once it is pushed onto the ramp it manages to start on an uphill run. Seems a bit strange.'

'We need to find the passengers. We have the ferry crew, just two men. The captain was inside the whole time, steering the vessel and the deckhand was amongst the passengers but he is a little vague. We'll go see them after this. We're also trying to get a proper ID on the victim. We have run the number plates but they belong to another car, owned by a couple in Inverness. They reported them stolen yesterday evening.'

'I'll book my hotel now,' said Hope. 'I could do with a bit of work away from things back in Glasgow.'

'Bit rough, was it? You okay, I mean,' Macleod went into a whisper, 'if there's anything you need away a while for, you can say. You've given a lot to the job over the last year; it owes you some slack.'

'I'm good,' said Hope, but Macleod was not convinced.

Stepping off at the Nigg side of the Firth, the pair walked along to the ferry and stopped short of the slipway. There was a cordon behind them and a small crowd was ogling, wondering at the sudden death in their midst. Macleod grabbed a hold of one of the forensic team and asked for their boss. But a voice interrupted him.

'Detective Inspector, if you're hanging around for a briefing, I'm sure I can help.' It was Hazel Mackintosh, the leader of the forensic team and someone Macleod had inadvertently offended the last time he was on the Black Isle. She was standing in her white coverall staring at him with her dark, thick-rimmed glasses. Macleod walked over and forced a smile. She had annoyed him last time but he was determined to make a bridge this time.

'Good to see you, Mackintosh. In your own time for the briefing—I'm sure you have plenty to do.'

'For you, Detective Inspector, I will always make room.'

It was all very forced, and Macleod thought it must look absurd to anyone else looking in, but it kept them both civil and cordial. Mackintosh led them away to a white shelter that had been erected and once inside called for some quiet. A number of her team exited and she pulled down her white hood, forcing a smile in the direction of Macleod.

'We have swept the ferry and the car, Macleod, and in truth it's not that positive from an identification point of view.

There are a lot of confused prints everywhere. We'll try to match them but it's going to take time, and then there's no guarantee that they are from anyone on this journey and not a previous one.'

'Anything from the car?' asked Hope.

'Well, that's another strange one. We are checking the chassis number to see if that yields anything. In terms of fingerprints, the car is incredibly clean. We have a few hairs and some skin samples but whether we can identify anything from them is debatable. They may belong to the deceased. What I can tell you is that he had a lot of cash in the boot, but hidden away in the side compartment. There are no ID or credit cards on him. Nothing to give away who he is or why he was here.'

'Someone on the run?' asked Macleod.

'Could be, sir. There's some rubbish in the well of the passenger seat. I'm guessing he stopped for something to eat. Might be worth going over CCTV in the local garages as it's branded packaging. He probably didn't get a chance to dump it.'

'And what about the victim,' asked Hope. 'Size, markings, haircut, anything?'

'He has the growth of at least a few days on his beard but his hair is cropped neatly and short. I'm guessing a military background but that's a hunch. Nails are trimmed too. What little was in the Jeep was stowed very neatly.

'In terms of his death, he was stabbed in the side. Very professional and meant to kill quickly, which it did. However, there's a complication.' Hazel Mackintosh looked over her thick-set spectacles and stared at Macleod. 'He was already dying.'

'How do you mean?' asked Hope.

'He had been poisoned. His body was paralysed when he was stabbed. He was completely immobile and I found the prick of where the poison was administered. We'll need to run tests to see what it is but it's very professional. Both actions are. Either someone got freaked that their first attempt was not working or this man was pissing off two separate parties.'

'Okay, is that everything?' asked Macleod.

'For now,' replied Mackintosh. 'You can go on deck and look around, I think we have most things, but just don't touch . . . and suit up, please.'

'Of course, and thank you, Mackintosh.'

'Detective Inspector.'

Macleod walked away and sought a suit to wear. When he realised that Hope was not following, he turned back and tapped her shoulder. 'You all right? I mean, are you? You're very distracted.'

'Fine, sir. Iain was military too.'

'If you need time . . .'

'I'm fine!' said Hope, too loudly to be fine. 'I'm good, sir.'

'Okay, but if you're not, say. Now suit up and let's take a look at this ferry. I'm going to call Allinson and get some CCTV checked at the petrol stations and services. Then we'll check out this ferry.'

Macleod made the call to Allinson but his eyes were on his partner who seemed out of sorts. He'd never seen her so down about a man, or about anything. Hope usually lived up to her name. After he had hung up, Macleod donned a suit of his own and joined Hope at the ramp of the ferry.

The vessel was quite simple. There was a loading area onto which cars could drive or reverse. The space was small and Macleod was impressed that they had managed to get three cars onto the deck. Beyond the open space was a cabin with a few seats and viewing windows. However, the view back to the cars was not extensive and Macleod believed it would be difficult to see the cars for the whole trip.

There was also another cabin, higher up, where the captain would pilot the vessel from. Everything looked normal. Around the craft were various pieces of safety equipment, bins for litter and posters indicating the dolphins and porpoises that could be seen occasionally from the vessel as it made its journey back and forth across the firth.

The Jeep was still covered and, looking underneath, Macleod saw the now bloodied seat left behind after the removal of the victim. If he was knifed as Mackintosh had said then the perpetrator would have opened the rear door to do it. When the poison was administered was up for debate. Until they knew how it acted, it could have been done at any time.

Walking off the ferry, Macleod pulled down his white overall hood and looked out to the water. 'This is not going to be an easy one, McGrath,' he said out loud. 'The kill was cold, calm, and quiet. We are looking at professionals of one sort or another. Hitmen or soldiers, I would guess. We need to tread carefully lest we end up on the wrong side of a bullet, or some other weapon.'

'Hitwomen, sir. Nothing to say it wasn't hitwomen.'

'Just an expression, Hope. Of course, it might have been the women. Or it might have been both. He was killed twice. Or at least two people had a go at it.'

Hope stood beside Macleod and joined him looking at the water of the firth. 'But until we get something else, we are pretty dead in the water, are we not?'

'True. Time to go see our ferrymen. And hope that the

footwork of the uniforms brings something in. Other than that, we have little except the method. And maybe a sketch or two.'

Chapter 4

The local hall at Cromarty was a hive of activity with police officers still setting up some areas whilst others were being used for interviews and statement taking. As Macleod walked in, he received nods and the occasional 'sir' from some officers while others were too deeply engaged. On the stage at the far end of the hall was Allinson, seemingly never off his mobile or radio. Macleod made his way up the small wooden steps onto the stage and stood, awaiting an ideal moment to interrupt his junior officer.

'Ah, sir,' said Allinson, spinning round and cancelling a call on his mobile. 'Your desk is over there and I have the latest updates in the folder on top of it. McGrath, yours is just across from the DI. Do you need anything right now, sir, or shall I leave you to it?'

'I need to speak to our ferrymen, Allinson. Can you get them here for an interview, I take it we have a quiet, secure area?'

'Yes, sir. I'll sort that for you now. Anything for you, McGrath?'

The man's tone was friendly, almost too much for a work environment, and it was distinctly different from the professional but cordial way he addressed Macleod. But Hope simply shook her head and wandered off to her desk. Macleod watched Allinson stare at her as she left but it was not a leer. Instead his face showed concern.

'Is she okay, sir?'

'She's here and working, Allinson. We have a job to do so let's get on with it.' He knew it was lame but he did not want to blurt out McGrath's personal problems to all and sundry. Besides, Allinson needed his focus as he was a lynchpin in the operation, co-ordinating everything, pulling it together while Macleod and McGrath went about solving the mystery.

Macleod was impressed that it took only five minutes before a coffee was on his desk. He had not asked for one, but such was the detail that Allinson invested himself in, Macleod never doubted it would arrive. It was brought by a young uniformed female officer who Macleod thought might have been on day release from a local college. It was just everyone had started seeming younger these days. The woman was probably at least twenty-three or something like that. He really was the grandfather of the force.

The officer had brought a map showing the locations of the nearby petrol stations and food shops where the driver of the Jeep may have bought his sandwiches. Uniformed officers were already going to these locations in order to establish if they had CCTV. It was a good line of enquiry. If the man was on the CCTV then he would not have been on the run from the police, as anyone worth their salt would not be so stupid. But on the run from others, then he might still go to such public places.

There were a few other reports, mainly witness statements of dog walkers who had seen the ferry depart and who might have seen the cars in question. The sketch artist was engaged with a number of the locals trying to put together images of the men and women Macleod was seeking. After reading these and realising his ferrymen had not yet arrived, he toured the room, saying hello to the team around him. It was good for morale, at least that was what the book said. Macleod reckoned it just stopped people making an arse of themselves by asking him who the boss was.

During this time, Hope remained at her desk and Macleod could tell she was not concentrating on the paperwork before her. A few times, he saw Allinson approach her and she seemed to be giving him a very cold shoulder. This was precious time he was using to reach her but she was clearly not appreciating it. He would need to keep an eye on the situation, as he needed them both on form.

Allinson tapped him on the shoulder as Macleod was talking to a junior officer and advised him the ferrymen were here. Hope was already on her way down from the stage and he intercepted her, motioning for her to stand to one side with him for a moment.

'Okay?' he asked.

'Yes!' Hope replied, a little too strongly.

'No, then. If you need the space, I'll release you. The force can run without you, Hope. This break-up has clearly had a big effect on you. And that's okay. Just say the word and you can go.'

Hope stared at him, her teeth grinding. 'I said I'm fine. Can we get on with it?'

Macleod nodded and then followed her to a room on the side of the hall where the two ferrymen were waiting. After shaking hands, Macleod asked for the deckhand to remain and called Allinson through to look after the captain of the vessel while they interviewed his colleague.

'I appreciate this must be a tremendous shock for you, sir, but we need to run over things again, so we can get on the trail of whoever did this.' Macleod saw the man was nervous, his hands shaking. 'How many runs had you made that morning, Peter? I am right in saying Peter?'

'Yes, I'm Peter. Peter Frasier. I think it was our fourth run of the day. To be honest they all blend in after a while.' He laughed nervously. 'Angus, that's the captain. He's also my uncle and got me the job on the ferry. You see I didn't do so well at school but this was a good job for me and I can do it. Uncle Angus says I do it well. Got my tickets and that.'

The man was trundling out words like they were about to expire so Macleod stepped in. 'Just slow down and take me through what happened on that fourth run. From the point where the cars got on the ferry.'

'Well, when we got over there was that Jeep and a Mini waiting to be picked up, and a third car behind them. So the Jeep reversed on. That's the way we prefer to do it, keep the hassle at the drive-on side as it means the other drivers waiting don't have to sit and watch someone making a hash of reversing off.

'So the Jeep reversed on without issue and then the Mini was going to simply reverse on and we'd be away. But there was a bit of commotion just beyond the slipway. There was one of those family cars, think they had kids in the back but hard to see well from the ferry. Anyway, there was an argument between them and these guys who have a car, but it was not in the queue. Was a smallish guy who was having a go at the dad through his car window. Well, I didn't see much else of that as I was helping reverse the Mini on but when I looked up, the family car was gone and there was this other car. A hatchback, these guys in the car.'

'Did you get a good look at any of them?' asked Macleod.

'No, sorry. I mean I did see them but I can't remember their faces. They walked past me and that and I saw them in the cabin but I don't recall them. I was more interested in the other car, the Mini.' The man looked down at his palms. 'There was this good-looking girl you see. And her mum wasn't bad too. Sorry, it's not that exciting going back and forth on the ferry. So, when someone you like steps on board you kinda look.'

'It's okay, Peter,' Macleod reassured, 'you're not on trial here. We just want to know what you know.'

'Well it was a squeeze getting this hatchback on but we did it and then I went inside due to the cold breeze and stared out of the window for the trip once I knew everyone was inside and I had done my quick safety brief.'

'Out of the window,' said Hope sharply. 'I don't believe you. You said you were eyeing up the girl.'

'Sorry! She was at the window, okay? I was looking out the window, or rather looking at her, looking out the window.'

'Thank you, Peter,' said Macleod, but his eyes were staring hard at Hope, giving a rebuke. 'Did you see what any of the passengers did in the cabin?'

'Not really. But the woman with the girl never came up to her. She threw me some glances, you know, the good ones where you look at each other but try not to catch each other looking. I thought I might have a chance.'

Hope went to speak but Macleod put his hand up to her and spoke instead. 'And then when you got to the other side?'

'Well, we were getting close and I called them all back to the cars. She was looking at me again but I had work to do so I got to the front of the vessel and got ready to sort out the ramp

27

and that. When I had that done, the hatchback drives off but the Mini was like stalling. The girl got out to push so I went to help. Her mum, or at least the other woman, who was pretty decent herself, stayed in the car. As we were pushing, trying to get the car going, someone got out of the rear. I now think there were three women in that car but I can't for the life of me think what the third one looked like.'

'Okay, Peter. And what happened then?' asked Macleod.

'Well, it was funny. We managed to push the car to the ramp and then onto the start of the slipway but it was not starting. I think the other woman might have got back in but I'm not sure as I had my head down pushing. But then the engine just started. I got a kiss on the forehead from the girl and then they were gone. Just like that.

'So I turned to the Jeep who had not made a sound during all of this, which I thought was unusual as people are usually arses when they get held up. But he didn't start the Jeep, so I went over and take a look. He's slumped on the wheel and then when I opened the door . . . '

'Go on,' said Macleod but the man was shaking now and Macleod could see tears welling up.

'Dead! He was bloody dead. Gutted, someone had gutted him, up into his ribs, like we gut a fish. The blood all down his side.'

'Easy,' said Macleod, 'it's okay. And you did what next?'

'Ran off the boat. It was pissing horrible. Blood, a lot of blood, all over my hand.'

Peter Frasier broke out into tears. He sniffed hard and Macleod stood up and came around the small table that separated them to put an arm on the young boy's shoulder.

'It's okay. Let it go, son.' Macleod looked back over the table but Hope was looking elsewhere. 'We'll get your uncle in here. Tell me, did you give descriptions to the sketch artist?'

'Yes, and what the girl was wearing. Had a flower badge thing. Did she do it? Did they? Was she just baiting me so I didn't see?'

'Calm down, Peter. This is not your fault.' But it was no use and Macleod shouted at Hope to get the boy's uncle.

After Peter Frasier had calmed down, Macleod interviewed his uncle but the captain of the vessel had little else to offer to illuminate the situation. He was out of the way and taking care of the vessel. He had given descriptions of people he had seen but it was all very vague.

The rest of the day was spent in compiling reports together that had been proffered by the local people. As they got into the later hours, Allinson came forward with a CCTV image of a vehicle and man buying a sandwich.

'We have a face, sir. It's vague but we should be able to do a search on it. I reckon it'll give quite a number of results so may I suggest I set the nightshift to it and we reconvene in the morning.'

Macleod nodded and yawned. 'I have my own digs up here. I was already up with Jane.' Macleod saw Allinson's questioning look. 'My partner, Allinson. We were taking in the place. I'm in a hotel in Inverness, the Railway Inn.'

'Very nice, sir. I'll contact you if there's anything in the night. Does McGrath have any arrangements?'

'Not that I'm aware of. Why? Did you book that place we had last time?'

'It is free, sir.'

'Okay, ask her then if she wants it. She has her own car with her anyway.'

Macleod gathered his things and as he went to leave, Hope returned to her desk. Watching her body language, Macleod saw a tired, frustrated woman who was putting up a brave but poor mask.

'Allinson booked the same place we had last time. Jane's in a hotel in Inverness so I'm going back to her tonight. Unless you need some company? You sure you are all right, Hope?'

'Yes, sir! Go! I'll be fine.'

The tone was insolent but Macleod let it go. She was clearly tired and annoyed but not with him. He gathered his belongings, including some case notes he would run through before morning. As he stepped outside and found his car, he saw Hope leave the building. She looked sullen and he thought better of annoying her again. But behind her, Allinson rushed out of the building.

'Are you okay? You seem a little down, McGrath. Do you want some company?'

'Yes!'

Macleod watched them depart. Hope striding ahead and Allinson desperately catching up after he had run back inside briefly. Macleod checked his watch. Midnight. *A good half hour back to the hotel and then back here for six in the morning. Five hours sleep maximum. And Jane to see as well. You need less sleep when you are old,* he thought. *Good job, too.*

Chapter 5

The alarm gave out its irritating electronic beeps, rushing one after another in a design that you could not help but react. You might flick the switch to off, bury yourself beneath a mass of duvet and pillows, or you might pull the device from its power source and fling it across the wall, but you would not stay still. Macleod groaned. Then he smelt her skin before him, and smiled. It was good to wake up with someone after twenty-odd years seeing the dawn on his own. He pulled Jane towards him and placed a kiss on the back of her neck.

'Is it that time already?' she moaned.

'I'm afraid so, but you can just stay here.'

'I'd make you breakfast,' Jane offered 'but the hotel staff might get annoyed with me in their kitchen. When we have the house, I'll get up and see you off, Seoras; don't doubt that.'

Macleod rolled out of his side of the bed and sought a pair of pants from his suitcase. They had only been there one night previous and all the clothes were in a suitcase. In the dark, Macleod struggled to find the pants and he had to wade through Jane's clothing which seemed to be more copious and generally at the top of the suitcase. He grabbed some underwear and went to step into it before realising that it was not his.

'How many clothes did you bring?' asked Macleod.

'Enough,' said Jane, quickly. 'Anyway, I don't know why I bring so much—all you want to do is get me out of them.'

Macleod smiled. The thought of Jane being out of her clothes was certainly a part of his pleasure but the real delight was in her quick and provocative barbs she threw in routinely. He loved it, almost like a naughty schoolboy used to like a look in the ladies' lingerie magazines. It was just that little bit rude, a spot of titillation to keep the day going.

'I'm sorry I was late back but it's just the start of the case. If you hadn't been asleep, I would have asked about your house hunting. Did you get anywhere?'

'I didn't get back to the hotel until nine. There were a lot to look at and quite far apart. But I saw one, Seoras, right down by the lochside, hidden away. There's a village nearby though and it's close to the road so we can pop to Inverness or wherever we want. It might take a bit of work though.'

The alarm bells rang in Macleod's head. 'How much work?'

'A bit but nothing too ridiculous. Look, you asked me to come up here with you; let me make a home for us.'

'I'm just not ready to do a lot of work to a place. I'm not that young anymore.' Now dressed, Macleod grabbed his bag and walked around the bed for the hotel room door. As he made for it, Jane threw back her covers and blocked his path. It caught his breath and he stood still as she wrapped herself around him.

'Trust me on this,' she whispered in his ear and then kissed the side of his neck. 'I'll sort out the details, you go catch some bad people. And be careful. I'll see you when I see you.'

Jane went to slink back to the bed but Macleod held her for

a moment, looking into her eyes. There was no concern or worry about what she proposed, just intrigue. For all that their relationship had been a whirlwind, he was looking forward to it being more settled. Although he doubted settled would ever mean dull.

'I need a study,' he said, 'nothing silly, just a small one. But I need one. Sometimes I need my space, even from you, Jane, as hard as I find that to believe.'

'And I need my space too,' she retorted. 'Don't worry, I'll find the perfect place. We'll each have what we need, and a massive bedroom in which you can ravish me repeatedly.'

There it was, that cheeky quip that was Jane. He smiled broadly as she laughed. 'I'll hold you to that.'

'Promises,' she giggled and he kissed her forehead, gently.

'I have to go. But let me know how you get on. On the mobile, photos and that. On one of those app things.'

'I'm not the technophobe, Seoras. Now go, before I'm forced to drag you back to my bed.'

Macleod let her go from his arms and watched her slip back under the covers, a moment of enjoyment before a busy day. As he walked out of the door his focus changed and he began to think through what he needed to do. Identify the victim, find the cars. It sounded simple but he knew it was really dependant on his team reaching out into the community and the CCTV of the land. Time to dive into the haystack and start looking.

Just over a half hour later, Macleod pulled up at the town hall they were using as their temporary base. There was very little parking but he had been reserved a space right outside the door. As he arrived, he saw Allinson approaching from the town side. He was wearing the same suit as yesterday which seemed unusual. Bit slack actually, Macleod thought he might have a word.

Allinson gave a nod and approached the car but Macleod pointed to the hall and held up his hand to indicate he would talk to him in five minutes time. As Allinson made his way inside, Macleod got out of his car and stretched his legs. But his eye caught movement further down the road. He could not mistake that figure, even if her head was down rather than showing her smiling demeanour.

It had not been that long since their escapade on the Isle of Harris where being a temporary stand in to their boss had almost cost Macleod and his partner their lives. McGrath in particular had been subject to several close calls. Since then Macleod had tried to keep an eye on her but she was missing something that she had before. That sparkle or vivacious approach to life she had was gone. It had been bothering him but he could not force his way in where she had not asked.

'Sir,' said McGrath as she reached the car.

'Morning, McGrath,' said Macleod as he was in ear shot of the officer on door duty. 'Sleep alright.'

'Yes, thanks. Jane okay?'

Macleod nodded and watched Hope go inside. But there had been something just as she replied. A flash of reflective enjoyment as he had asked if she slept well. He wondered if she had taken company last night. And then it clicked. Allinson, still in his old clothes. She had liked him on Lewis when they had first met. Macleod grinned. *Let's pray it's good for her.*

When he entered the building, he saw some tired faces, those who had been up in the night collating what had come in and who would be off to their bed shortly. Macleod grabbed a coffee and then made for his desk to await Allinson and the night cover making their handover. Hope pulled up a chair at the end of his desk and Macleod had to force himself not to ask how her night had been. His focus turned to the case as Allinson approached his desk.

Behind Allinson approached a figure Macleod recognised. DC Ross had been his main man during the last case on the Black Isle and he was obviously taking the night watch this time. Macleod stood up and shook the man's hand. 'What do you have, Ross? It's good to see you.'

'Morning, sir. Good to see you both as well. There's not a lot to add. We have been correlating the statements from the area and those who were there. Nothing on the cars except for the Jeep. It was stolen on the outskirts of Oban two days ago, so that's a waypoint for our victim. I've contacted the local station there and asked them to hunt for any CCTV close to where it was stolen. Also, we have footage of our man buying his sandwiches on the outskirts of Inverness. We've been checking the cameras there but apart from him buying his food we can't find anything linking to anyone on the ferry.

'We've run the facial recognition on our victim and we came up with a few hits. But we have just narrowed it down to a Malthe Amundsen. I have an address but it's a house on the Isle of Mull, pretty remote. I contacted the station on Mull but we have very few people there so we are sending over some reinforcements from Oban for them although if I'm honest, that's probably going to be maybe two people at most.'

Macleod nodded and rubbed his chin, giving himself a moment to think. 'McGrath, get ready to take a bag. I want you down at his house and to pass through Oban to coordinate things there. See if we can find out who he really is, what he's been doing, and why he seems to have run. What else do we have, Ross?'

'Not much, sir, although we are still engaging in the trawl for the other vehicles. We managed to piece together a partial number plate on the Mini but no joy finding it yet. Nothing from forensics on the poison used or the blade that killed Malthe. However, Mackintosh did say she was expecting to brief you later this morning. She's been up all night at her lab, so she must be close to something.'

Ross then ran through the smaller details of where the uniform teams were working. Once he had finished, Macleod stood up and sat on the end of his desk looking at his three DCs.

'I think we're about to become a little thin on the ground as this investigation is now across the country. So as I said, I'm sending McGrath down to Mull. I want you with her, Allinson, in case we need to drop one of you in Oban or to remain in Mull. That's a long trail up to here, so we need to make sure we get as much detail as we can from Malthe's travels.

'Ross, I need you here, sitting over the top of the information gathering. I know you've been up all night but can you get a sleep and then be back here before midday? I'll cover here until then.'

Ross looked a little put out but Macleod put that down to his being up all night. As the three of them rose from their seats, Macleod called Hope over.

'Are you okay this morning?' he asked.

'Fine. Sleep did me good.' There was no trace of anything but a polite reply.

'If you need to investigate outside of Mull or Oban, don't be afraid to drop Allinson and you cover the new leads. We're using a lot of manpower up here so I don't think

36

we'll have much to spare down there. I doubt we'll get anything substantial from inquiries here as this seems to be premeditated and possibly a hit. So we need to dig up this guy's past and present. Who was he? Who didn't like him? Why did he run? What sort of life did he lead? How long was he in Scotland and in Mull particularly? You know the drill.'

'Sure. I'll just pop back and grab a bag for the car and then get going. Ross can have the keys to the digs we have here, then he won't be travelling back and forward.'

Hope turned away and Macleod watched her go. When he had first met her his eyes would have watched that figure with pleasure but now all he felt was concern. She was not herself. Part of his decision to send Allinson with her was his gut instinct that said they had been together last night and he had helped her. In what capacity that was he tried not to think too closely about. Hope had become his right arm when it came to the job and he struggled to remember working without her despite them having been together barely a year.

Macleod spent the rest of the morning cajoling his team in the hall, running over statements and reports from the wide investigation that was underway. He briefed the room just after ten and then took a short walk around Cromarty to keep his head clear and once again look at the slipway. They had opened up the Cromarty side but the ferry still sat berthed on the Nigg side of the Firth. He saw the coffee house was open and decided to grab himself a drink. Inside, the cosy building was packed with dog walkers and locals. Gina Walker was serving at the till and he saw Gerrard Bean the owner working the large machine.

'Inspector, good morning, do you want me, or is it a coffee?' asked Gina.

'I actually came in for a coffee but now that you mention it, I could do with you for a few minutes, if Mr Bean can spare you.'

'Certainly Inspector, I'll just come now.'

Macleod held up his hand. 'A latte first please. And one for yourself.'

Gina smiled and briefly went behind the serving bar to talk to her boss. She told Macleod to wait outside and she'd be out presently with their drinks. The air was warm as Macleod stepped out into sunshine, a significant change from the day before. Wandering down to the slipway, he stared at the water. They needed something from this lead in Mull. He needed to know the victim, his past. But he also needed to know something about the other passengers. It was frustrating and he felt he had his hands tied behind his back, searching for reasons for murder without knowing any of the suspects. But it would come; he needed to be patient.

'Here you go, Inspector.'

Macleod turned around and took the cup Gina was presenting to him. The steam from the coffee made him smile. Tasting it, he nodded his approval. 'Very good; you're obviously not some philistines out to make a mint.'

'No,' said Gina laughing. 'Gerrard's very particular about his coffee. So, what can I do for you, Inspector? I don't want to be too long as you can see it's very busy today. Everyone wants the gen on what happened.'

'It's been a short while since the incident and sometimes things come back to people, often little insignificant moments or ideas but at times they are very important. I just wanted to check by and see if you had any other thoughts about the people you saw.' Macleod watched the girl look blankly at him and then try to think. 'Your sketch with the artist was very useful by the way.' This was so far a lie but he wanted to encourage her, and who knew, it might be very valuable as the case went on.

'I don't think so, Inspector. I was trying to think through things last night, try and bring things to mind, but you start to doubt yourself if you try too hard. You imagine things.'

Macleod sipped his coffee and looked out at the sea. 'That's undoubtedly true on occasion but don't worry about that. My job is to sift through the detail and work out what is correct. Your job is simply to remember as vividly and as accurately as you can.'

'I understand. But really there's nothing further.'

'What about accents? The man who came in to the cafe for the coffee, what was his voice like?'

Gina turned her face up as if to show she was mulling over the question but Macleod was not hopeful. 'I said it was proper English but when I heard him speak outside the building, it was a different accent.'

'Scottish?'

'Oh, no. Definitely not a Scottish accent. I mean none of our accents. Certainly not local and not Glasgow or Edinburgh in tone. He was definitely not a native speaker.'

'Macleod felt a rush and pressed on. 'What makes you say that?'

'Now you've put the question that way I'm thinking what the accent is not. It was funny in some ways because there was not a lot of accent there. And remember, I did not have many words to play with.'

'Was it African?' Macleod doubted this but it was very extreme to what he guessed the accent might have been and this would help give Gina further confidence.

'Oh, no. Not African. Not Australian, or anything that way. Not American either, or Canadian. No, it was definitely Europe. Not Irish though, or Italian or Spanish.'

'Russian, perhaps?'

'No,' replied Gina emphatically. 'Maybe Swedish but it was very light, not a heavy accent, in fact quite flat.'

Macleod grabbed his mobile and pulled up a video app, searching for Danish accents. A video soon played and he turned up the volume.'

'Yes,' said Gina, 'like that. That's it, it's quite subtle really, isn't it? Is that Swedish?'

'No,' said Macleod but he was now looking out at the water and his mind racing. 'It's Danish, Miss Walker, definitely Danish, flatter than Swedish or Finnish, I'm told.'

'That's new on me.'

'Maybe so, but that is most helpful. Most helpful indeed.'

Chapter 6

The day seemed long to Macleod after Hope and Allinson departed. It was one of waiting, trawling evidence and reports gathered in from the surrounding area. Given the Danish connection he had sent communications to the Danish police force asking for any information they had on the deceased man. He also sent the sketch of the man in the cafe over to see if that drew any leads. The local uniform section were out pounding the doors and checking the various garages and cafes looking for sightings of any of the three cars.

Ross arrived at midday and took over the minute-to-minute running of the room so Macleod took a stroll and picked up some lunch in the small cafe in the town. With Hope travelling down, he had no one to chat with and he decided a call to Jane would be best. Her hunt was going well and she had seen many more houses.

'You know, I thought I was just following you up here but the place kind of grows on you. It's very peaceful, with the number of forests and mountains. Even in winter it must look spectacular. I guess you are just used to it.'

'I'm not from here,' said Macleod, 'I just used to travel down the A9 a lot in earlier days, mountains lining the road. It'll be a change for me again after so many years in the city. Although Inverness is becoming a real city, too. But we want something out of the way. I'm getting less inclined towards people, want my space.'

'And you shall have it. I think we can probably afford something of a reasonable size. You won't need to see me all day, maybe just a small fraction of it.' Her voice had dipped and Macleod panicked.

'I didn't mean it like that.' And then he heard the laugh.

'You need to read me better, it's like shooting fish in a barrel. How do you catch anyone in your game?'

Macleod's mood had lifted as he made his way back to the hall that was serving as a communications base. As he approached, his mobile was ringing. He looked down and saw Ross's number. Being only a few hundred yards from the hall, he ignored the phone and quickened his pace. On entering, he spied Ross on the stage area and called to him.

'A body, sir,' shouted Ross. 'Up in Embo, Dornoch way. On the beach at a holiday park. Was called in to the coastguard. I managed to get a photograph, which showed a flower badge, and show it to Peter Frasier on the ferry. He confirmed it as the girl he spoke to.'

'Stay here Ross, I'll go. I take it we have someone already up there.'

'Yes sir, two officers on scene and they are using the Coastguard to help protect the area.'

'Perfect, get Mackintosh up there with her team, and some backup if we have it.' Macleod spun around and looked at his team around him. Despite having spent the morning talking to most of them, he had no idea of names, his Achilles heel. He pointed at a young woman who was taking incoming calls with another man.

'What's your name, officer?'

'Ross, sir.'

Macleod looked up at his DC on the stage and raised questioning eyes. The man shook his head. 'Macleod turned back to the female officer. 'Okay, you're with me. And you're driving. You know how to get to Embo, up at Dornoch?'

'Yes, sir.'

Macleod reached into his pocket and grabbed his keys, throwing them over to the officer. 'Blue hatchback outside. I'll be with you directly.'

'Was there anything else while I was out, Ross?' asked Macleod to his officer on the stage.

'Only that we had a sighting of the Mini at a cafe in Kessock, yesterday prior to the incident. No CCTV but we have a partial number plate and that might make up a whole one. Working on that. Two females and then a third one joining them. Getting descriptions and sketches sorted. I'll update when we have, sir.'

'Good, Ross. Hold it together here. And thanks for stopping on with so little sleep.'

Ross nodded and Macleod left the building, getting into the passenger side of his car, the engine already running.

'What's your first name, Ross?' asked Macleod. 'I can't be doing with two Rosses in the same room.'

'There's three of us, sir, but I'm Hayley. Recently moved up. I was a special constable for a while and then took the plunge. There weren't many jobs going and with my poor exam—'

Macleod held up his hand. 'I'm sure your life history is fascinating, Hayley, but right now I need to think. So next time we have some down time tell me all, I mean that. But, and forgive me, just shut up and drive for now. And make it quick.'

She didn't seem to take offense and Macleod felt genuinely sorry for her. She was excited but he needed to think. *So you kill someone on a ferry, probably targeted. Then you go north and dispose of the only one to get out of the car, or at least the only one identifiable. Possible they met in a cafe in Kessock, so not long there. It sounds like a disposable person. Bad choice of friend, dear, very bad choice.*

The drive up was uneventful and Macleod pondered on the details he had as the views of the sea on one side measured up against the mountains skirting the road on the other side. He saw distillery houses, a small port and houses looking out at this majesty. Many houses, or so it seemed to Macleod, said 'For Sale' on them and he fought to stop thinking about his possible move.

As they drove through Dornoch, he checked his mobile for details of the scene of the death and directed his younger colleague to Embo and then along to a holiday park. As they drove in, he could see the place was buzzing with activity, visitors to the site, talking incessantly and all huddled towards a cordon at the far end of the site.

There was a line of people in blue jumpsuits and Macleod saw the jackets that stated 'Coastguard Rescue'. With the car parting the tide of onlookers by the road, Macleod flashed his credentials and pointed Constable Hayley Ross to a gathering at the end of the holiday park.

As they parked, Hayley looked at Macleod. 'Not being funny, sir, but I'm not long in. I'm normally behind the desk answering telephones and pushing leads that way. Have been out on the street but never at a murder scene. What do you want from me?'

'Then you are in luck. Time to learn, Hayley. Keep your eyes open and don't be afraid to ask questions. And if you need a moment when you see the body, that's fine, just don't make a fuss.'

With that, Macleod exited the vehicle and strode to a concrete pier that extended to the sea. At the end of it he had seen a dark blue uniform and he wanted an update. Behind him he heard the scrambling feet of Hayley which broke into an easier stride as she caught up with him.

'Constable,' said Macleod, extending a hand to the officer on scene, 'DI Macleod, Constable Ross with me. Give me a briefing, please, on the situation.'

'Yes, sir. Constable Anderson. Together with Constable Mackenzie, we proceeded to a report of a body found in the water. It was called in by a Britney Mathews, eighteen-year old, up here on holiday. She called the coastguard and we were informed. The station officer of the coastguard is over there, name of Dunwoody, and his senior officer just arrived. I believe he's briefing him as I am you.

'Britney was walking along the shore after an argument with her sister, they are up on holiday, and saw the body floating in the water. The coastguard came and retrieved the casualty, treating the situation as a live person. They began CPR but there was no response. Helicopter came and the casualty was confirmed deceased by their paramedic. I requested that the body remain for our scenes of crime as instructed by DC Ross from your team, sir. Mackenzie is with the first informant but I doubt she will be of much use. Paramedic reckoned the casualty had been dead for hours.'

'Thank you, Anderson. I'll talk to the coastguard and see

45

what I can garner but let's have a look at the body.'

'This way, sir.' Constable Anderson led Macleod and Hayley past two Coastguard officers to the body of a blonde-haired girl, maybe late teens who was lying on her back. She wore dungarees and there was a yellow flower badge pinned onto them. Macleod bent down to examine the body as best as he could without touching it.

'Something round the back here. Ross, get your gloves on,' said Macleod. He snapped a pair of his own on and then beckoned Hayley to come closer. 'I need you to lift the body up a bit. I think there's a wound in here, through the dungarees.' His colleague obliged and Macleod found a tear through the denim and saw a gaping wound. 'Knife of some sort.'

'So, she was killed and dumped into the water.'

'That's a theory, Mackintosh will give me a better idea but this poor girl looks like she was disposed of. I reckon she's not even well known to her killers. Rather, she was a good decoy for the ferry. It's looking like the ladies did the knifing on the ferry. The men were somewhat more subtle. Still doesn't give a lead on them. Hopefully they have been lazy and SOCO can get something. Doubt it though. We need the Kessock lead to come through with some IDs.'

Macleod stepped away and removed his gloves. He wandered over to the Coastguard senior officer and shook hands. 'DI Macleod. And?'

The man opposite was at least six foot and then some, broad and the proper look of a hero. He had to be in the line of rescue work. But beyond him, Macleod saw the many shapes and ages of the coastguard volunteers.

'Hume. SCOO, Senior Coastal Operations Officer. I take it you're happy with the team's actions.'

Macleod nodded. 'Thank you for staying around and keeping the scene. We are pretty stretched but we have people on the way. Looking at the body, you may not have had a chance to rescue her. I believe the paramedic was of the same opinion.'

Hume agreed. 'Yes, poor girl was long gone. Do we have an ID, or any detail on what she was doing?'

'Under investigation at this time. Your guys can do modelling of the tides and that, can you not? If I said she was probably entering the water during last night or evening can you give a rough area where she would have entered?'

'It'll be rough but yes. Let me make a few calls and see what we can turn up.'

Macleod walked back to Hayley Ross who was taking some photographs. 'Just sending some more images back to the DC at base.'

Macleod found himself hanging on awaiting Mackintosh and her team. His companion kept him busy with little questions about the scene and the girl but really, she was asking things that Macleod had long gone over in his head. But he didn't want to stop her, as he was like that once. But there was no doubt the arrival of Mackintosh was a relief.

'It's all yours, Mackintosh, he said as she arrived. When and how, please.' He was about to leave when Hume came up to him.

'Inspector, about the passage of the body in the water. It's hard to model given the coastline but according to the local knowledge, she would not have been far from here, indeed maybe here. Certainly, a mile of so either side, at most, is the thought. Hope that helps.'

Macleod thanked the man, said his goodbyes where necessary and then instructed Hayley to drive him back to Cromarty. As they departed Embo, Macleod's mobile rang.

'Sir,' said DC Ross as Macleod placed the mobile to his ear, 'the Mini has been spotted by a passer-by. North of your location by about five miles. Hidden in some woods. I'm texting you further details.'

'I'm going Ross. Is it on the coast road?'

'Yes, sir.'

'Right then, send me those details.' Macleod turned to his female colleague driving the car. 'Hayley, take the road to the right and keep at a normal speed. They've found the Mini. But we need to be quiet approaching. We can't blow this.'

Chapter 7

Hayley drove the car steadily but at the maximum legal speed along the coastal road. Macleod tried not to stare out of the window but still keep an eye on the surrounding scenery, looking for the Mini. His mobile was sitting on his lap, awaiting DC Ross's text, updating the position.

'That's good, Hayley,' he said to his driver, 'nice and steady. If I spot it, don't stop suddenly. We'll go slightly past and get off the road so we can approach. Unfortunately, you're not going to be very inconspicuous in that uniform.'

'Yes, sir.' Hayley Ross was shaking underneath her forced exterior. It was obvious to Macleod and he felt for her. Remembering his first chases in Glasgow and how handling the adrenalin was the easy part, the nervous excitement and mild terror of what might come being the more difficult side of the coin.

His mobile vibrated. Macleod never had his mobile issue a sound, preferring to keep it quiet and he suddenly thought of Hayley's radio.

'Remember to turn the volume down on your radio when we get out, Constable. It's just past Dunrobin Castle, left hand side, this side of a train track.'

Five minutes later, Macleod spotted the black and white Mini and he pointed to the roadside up ahead, telling Ross to pull the car into a small lay-by. On exiting, he saw the railway line beyond the trees at the side of the road and decided that this would be a better approach than walking back along the road. Motioning to Ross, he climbed a wire fence and cut past a hedge and several trees to the railway line.

'Keep tight to the edge, Hayley. Looks like a proper train track, so we might get one to come along.' Inside, Macleod could feel the stomach tighten. He picked up his mobile and called Ross, reporting his position and action, requesting all backup to approach silently. After a few minutes' walk, he could see the Mini, and he halted, crouching down to the hedge beside the track, looking for any signs of movement.

'There's a building over the tracks,' said Hayley. 'It looks derelict, broken windows and that. Could be a place for someone.'

'True,' said Macleod. 'We'll cross the tracks here and make into that field so we can approach from behind the hedge. Be careful. Hayley, these people are killers, and I doubt they would hesitate to use lethal force on us given what they have done so far.'

And there it was. When he mentioned lethal force, he felt that numbing reality he rarely got. Most murder cases did not involve a situation like this. He thought about waiting for back up but he could lose his lead if he stayed still.

Macleod crossed the tracks and then waved Hayley over behind him. She had drawn her nightstick and looked better equipped for the fight than he did. Hopefully, it would not come to that. They needed to get close and see if anyone was there but he was wary of getting too near. If these people were killers . . .

'I'm just going a little further forward, Hayley. You stay here. Backup is on the way. We'll just make sure they don't run off if they are here.' Macleod held his hand up to reinforce his point. It was a lot to ask of a new constable and he hoped he was keeping her safe by doing this. It was one thing to risk himself but he did not know if Hayley could handle herself. She was not the fittest-looking constable he had ever seen, not that physique was the measure of a police officer. Intelligence was often much more useful.

Macleod crept forward and slid up against the wall of the derelict house. Inside he could hear voices, one was in pain. There seemed to be an argument going on.

'Bloody great timing. What the hell is wrong with you?'

'I don't know,' winced another voice. 'It feels like an appendix or something; it's fucking killing me.'

'You've had the paracetamol, just bite down on it. Keep it stum or we'll have the rest of the world in here.'

'You need to move me,' said the second voice. Both were female but the first was distinctly deeper than the second.

'You'll just have to grin and bear it. I'll try and get you to somewhere.'

'Quist's still up this way. He was a decent medic; he might be able to do it. Nah, forget that. Get me to a pissing hospital.'

'No way, we are going nowhere public; you don't know who saw us on that ferry. We need to ditch the car and get a new one and then get south. Then you can get into a hospital. In fact, better still, get you out of the country and then get to a hospital.'

'If it's a fucking appendix, then I'll die, you idiot. Get me some help now. And no bloody horse doctor either.' There was a brief silence and the same voice spoke. 'We'll find Quist. He'll help us. Me and Quist had some good romps together. He was better than the Sarge anyway.'

Macleod heard a police car siren in the distance and the conversation inside dramatically came to a close. He heard footsteps and then a door opened somewhere. His heart began to pound. If they came around the house he was wide open. He needed cover and fast. But there was very little.

The police siren got louder as it came closer and Macleod ducked down to the ground, readying himself to spring up if detected. He heard some footsteps and then the rustle of a hedge. The siren was now only a few hundred yards away and was starting to obscure the local sounds. The rustle was gone and Macleod swung his head back and forth scanning the area as quickly as he could. Then he heard a cry.

It came from Hayley's direction and he saw the young woman suddenly stand up straight as someone grabbed her from behind and looked like they were driving a knife into her back several times. Macleod yelled and looked around him for a weapon. He saw a rock and after grabbing it, flung it hard at the assailant who seemed to be struggling with their knife.

His throw was a good one and caught the attacker on the head. There was a swear and then the woman fought with something in Hayley's back before letting her fall to the floor as Macleod arrived. The attacker had a scarf around her face but her blonde hair, tied in a ponytail swung as she stepped forward and jabbed a hand at Macleod's face. It was faster than the 'Glasgow punches' he was used to and although he threw his head back, he was caught on the chin and sailed off his feet landing on the ground, his chin screaming in agony.

Throwing his hands up in front of him to prepare for the next blows, Macleod was surprised to find no follow up arriving. Instead, he heard the attacker run off. He tried to get to his feet but he was unsteady and decided to go to Hayley rather than continue pursuit.

'My back! Something went in my back,' screamed Hayley.

Macleod spun the woman over and saw the blood on the back of her shirt. He had to spin her back over to undo her stab vest and then back again to take it off. Her shirt was sodden with blood and he pulled it up to see two wounds in her back, both leaking blood. Macleod took off his jacket and laid it on Hayley.

'I'll be back, hold on, just keep it together. Please keep it together.'

The last was said as he grabbed Hayley's radio and switched the volume up, running for the car. He crossed the railway line as he contacted the operator on the main setting, requesting more backup and an ambulance. As he reached the car, he saw the Mini drive off along the main road and he noted the number plate relaying it to the operator on the radio. Then he grabbed the first aid box from the rear of the car and raced back to the railway line. As he came through the hedge, he felt the vibration and flung himself back into the hedge. A train whipped past inches from his face.

'Come on,' screamed Macleod as he watched it past. Once it was clear, he ran back to Hayley and tore out bandages and applied pressure to the wounds.

'Are you still with me? Hayley, are you still there?'

'Yeah, still here. Can't seem to get any momentum though.'

Macleod heard a laugh and he thought that maybe the injuries were not so bad. Or maybe they were and she was just delirious. A police car screamed past reminding Macleod of the first siren he had heard. Where had they gone? This new one was in pursuit, as he had just called it in but what was the first one all about?

'You'll be fine, Ross, stay with me.' The conversation was automatic, part of the training, keeping an injured party talking, keeping them conscious as best you could. *Where's the damn ambulance? I could do with Hope; she's better at this sort of thing than me.*

He saw a walker go past on the main road and started screaming to the man. Thankfully he did not run off but came through. 'Go out there and if you see an ambulance, you wave your arms and flag it down for here, sir. Understand me?'

The man nodded and disappeared back though the hedge as Macleod kept talking to his colleague, asking her questions about the case. *And who were these people that they simply attacked a police officer? Thank God for stab vests.*

Macleod heard the ambulance and was pushed aside a few minutes later as a man clad in green started to work on Hayley. Macleod stepped back as another paramedic joined in. Shortly, he saw a coastguard team arrive and help stretcher Hayley out to the ambulance as the place was shrouded in police. After giving instructions for the area to be cordoned off and that no one was to enter, he went to the ambulance to check on Ross.

'We're underway in a moment, boss,' said the paramedic. 'Do you require any treatment?'

'No, just a sore jaw,' said Macleod. 'How is she?'

'She's fine, or rather will be. Those wounds are not that deep and they certainly didn't do any serious damage or I would not be hanging around. She's in shock though. So, we'll take her in and she'll get tidied up and probably kept in for the night. Bloody big blade on the ground though—she was lucky.'

Macleod thanked the man and stepped away from the ambulance and watched it depart. They had both been lucky. He grabbed the radio and called control asking for an update on the escaping Mini. It was on fire at the roadside, in a layby of other cars. *Dammit, they stole another one. They're gone,* thought Macleod. He looked at the derelict building through the hedgerow. *You need to tell us something, or we are stuffed.* And then he remembered what the woman had said. *Quist . . . we need to find Quist.*

Chapter 8

L eaving Oban, Hope stood on the outside deck of the ferry and stared at the island across the bay. She had been this way only once before and, if truthful, she did not remember much about that visit as she was only a child. But she recognised the rugged scenery all along the west coast of Scotland, the rising hills in the distance, swathed in green, and the cold waters which provided a livelihood to many.

The ferry made its way out of the bay and she could see Mull in the distance. But all around, she saw islands and parts of the mainland that jutted out into the sea forming the sounds and channels. She often thought about hiring a boat and simply cruising around with someone on a lazy holiday in these parts. And the sun was always shining in these dreams as they sat bronzing themselves on the deck in utter solitude, breaking the day with only that most intimate of exercise. She had wanted to do this with him.

But he was gone, and she had a case to get on with. The drive down from Inverness to Oban had been a quiet one, with Allinson slipping on the radio and only occasionally asking her some light questions. Mentioning the case, they had a discussion of five minutes—their longest of the journey. But there was another tension in the air.

She had not been fair to him. In her hour of need, of wanting someone close to hold and tell her how important and gorgeous she was, he had stepped up to the mark. He had been everything she had needed both in and out of the bed. And she had been a wall of silence. She was giving him some shitty treatment and she knew it.

'You okay?' Hope did not look round but merely nodded her head. 'I know the scenery's good but you're staring so hard at it, I might doubt you had ever seen land.'

It was not that funny a comment but Hope smiled at a man who was trying his best to understand and help her. She should give him a way in because he had been exceptional and dedicated, but she was not in the mood. It was not her fault; it was that other bastard.

'Do you want anything, McGrath? I'm going to get a drink.'

'Just space,' said Hope. *Hell, that was harsh.*

'Okay, I'll be downstairs.'

'Allinson, I'm sorry; it's just I need a little space. Sorry, you've been great, and it was great.'

He nodded and walked away. Hope could tell she had hurt him. For a moment she hesitated, ready to turn back to her scenery and punishing contemplation of the ruins of her life. But then she saw the one good thing of the last few days walking away and ran after him. Grabbing his shoulder, she turned Allinson around. His face seemed bemused and she took his hand.

'Sorry. I'm not saying I'm done with you. I didn't just use you because I needed a warm pair of arms. But I need time to get rid of the guy before you. I have no right to ask but please, hang in there.' Hope rubbed his hand and sought reassurance in his face.

'Okay. I'll do my best, McGrath. But you're not giving me a chink of light to see by.'

'Hope. Call me Hope.'

He smiled and then walked away, down the stairs to the lower deck. Hope prayed the man had enough faith in her to stay interested because she had so little to give out at the moment. She had not had many relationships and she was not sure she wanted any more after how the last one had left her feeling.

A short while later, Allinson drove their car off the ferry at Craignure, and navigated to the south side of the island. The address was indicating a home at the Ross of Mull, a piece of land that had a small island just off it where tourists took the ferry to see the monastery of Iona. But the house they were looking for was on a dirt track that split off from the main road about a mile before Fidden and the small ferry terminal.

The building had been searched quickly and then taped over awaiting specialists from the mainland. Hope and Allinson had made it before the forensic team had arrived. They donned their gloves and then tore back the tape on the door which was lying slightly ajar.

'They said they hadn't touched anything,' remarked Allinson.

'Well, he must have been in a hurry if he left his door open.' Hope looked around the countryside from the front door. 'But he's so far off track, you would not hear anything.'

Pushing the door open, Hope stepped inside to a sparse hallway. There were no pictures or decorations on the wall, just a beige wallpaper that had seen better days. The house was a bungalow and there were only three rooms off the hallway. Hope took the first one on offer and found herself in a lounge that had been knocked through to a kitchen behind. Again, the room was sparsely decorated, a wood stove dominating the room. There was a small sofa, a drinks cabinet, a bureau, and a computer desk. But there was no television, no radio, and very little else.

'Not much of a party animal,' said Allinson. 'And a computer desk with no computer. He's got a printer and speakers though.'

'Looks like a laptop docking station. We didn't find anything in the car. Why take your laptop and then not have it with you in your car as you travel? Might be important.' Hope was talking to the air in a way she could not do with Macleod. Now she was senior officer, she didn't feel the need to pass all her thoughts to her boss.

'Not much food in the kitchen,' said Allinson, opening a few cupboards and the fridge. 'But there's dirty pans in the sink. Maybe he was disturbed. Seems to be the story being told.'

Hope made her way through to the bedroom and looked at a single camp bed in a bare room. The carpet made the place look like a squatter's den. That and the two bottles of whisky lolling around on the carpet, both empty.

'Hope, come through to the other room; you need to see this!' shouted Allinson.

Making her way to third room, Hope gasped as she entered. It was the utility room but the place was a mess. There was blood on the wall and many items had been knocked to the ground. The washing machine door was covered in red as if someone had smashed their head off it. The window, too, was smeared in blood. Carefully, Hope scanned the room, looking for anything significant but she could not find anything.

'Is there anything else to this abode?' asked Hope.

'Shed out the back; I saw it on the way in. It's nothing much, looks very run down.'

'Let's take a look.'

They exited the bungalow through the front door and walked around to the rear. Some two hundred metres away was a rough-looking shack that some may have called a shed. Hope was keen to call it a ruin. She could see two indentations in the ground either side of the shed and wondered why the ground was undulating in such a regular pattern at these points. Elsewhere it just seemed to roll here and there as it chose, rising and falling at random.

Allinson arrived at the shed first and Hope saw him wheel around the ground in front of the door. 'Wet patch there and what looks like the remnants of a footprint but it's hard to tell. I'll leave that for forensics.'

Hope agreed and skirted the area too as Allinson opened the shed door. Hope followed him inside and they found themselves tight up against each other as they tried to take in the items in the tight space. There were tools, most of which looked like they had been hanging there for years. Allinson reached for one and it fell apart in his hands which became covered in rust.

'Who keeps somewhere like this?' he said. 'It's bloody manky. Do you think he ever came out here?'

'Yes,' said Hope, firmly. 'Look at the floor, very dusty, almost undisturbed except for the lines between the wooden boards. Except it's not all of them, just a few. Have you a pen knife, Allinson?'

'Yes, here.'

Taking Allinson's knife, Hope ran it down the gap between the floorboards and found that only on three gaps did it sink down into the floor. At the others it stopped, showing a depth of only a few millimetres. Hope sighed.

'It's all an illusion, Allinson. This is false, meant to keep the casual onlooker at bay. Give me one of the chisels off the shelf there, but one that isn't going to fall apart in my hands.'

With care, Hope took the chisel and again ran down one of the cracks in the boards, one where the pen knife had dropped down through the gap. Once she was happy she had the chisel in place, she pushed down, levering the board which fought momentarily before lifting up. Allinson joined in and lifted the board up and clear. Hope reached over and lifted the other side up and they looked down into a small hide that held a number of weapons.

'Bloody hell,' said Allinson. 'This guys a right Rambo. Look at this stuff; you don't buy that off the local DIY shelf.'

'There's grenades there, too. We'd better call ordnance when we get clear. Some of the stuff is missing though. But not much, given the space.'

'Maybe he didn't have time,' suggested Allinson.

'Well, someone has disturbed him and he's dealt with them to some degree and then grabbed some weapons and run. That's how it looks. There's no car and he's in a stolen one once he's got to the mainland. Someone wanted our man, wanted him bad. Maybe two sets of people, but then who are these people?'

'Too many questions, Hope.'

'I wonder where these came from,' said Hope, pointing at the weapons. 'It might help but I reckon his laptop is what we really want. Maybe he had more hides around here.'

'Did you see the land around here? There's a bit of symmetry, either side of this shed. Looks like the land was dug down. We should check that out.'

'Agreed,' said Hope. 'You go and check them out. I'll get on the blower to ordnance. I'm just going to walk away a distance before ringing. Not sure I'll get a signal anyway—might need to use the radio.'

Walking away from the shed, Hope found that there was indeed no signal. She had to return to the car and use her handheld radio, calling in the situation and asking for assistance from the explosives division of the military and for more officers to come and stand guard on the site once they had left.

As she was on the radio, she watched Allinson walking over to the dip on the right of the shed. He had to walk over three hundred yards and when he arrived, she saw him bend down and start to unscrew something. A few minutes later, he was throwing a large metal circle to one side and reaching down into the ground. She saw him struggle but she was still talking to base and was unable to go over and help. After a few minutes, he stood up and waved his hands at her.

'Yes,' shouted Hope, holding the radio to one side.

'There's a radio here, and other communications devices that I don't recognise fully. But it all looks like things to let you talk to people. Some serious shit here, Hope.'

'Excellent!' she shouted back. 'Make a note of them and leave them alone unless you recognise how to work any, or if they have any documentation with them. Then note that down.'

She watched Allinson nod and then return to the hole in the ground. As she came off the radio to base, she saw him replacing the cover on the hole. It was a good idea in case of rain. As Hope made her way from the car, Allinson made his way back to the house and across to the second dip they had seen.

His figure was quite something—at least it had been the night before and now as evening was setting in, Hope let herself enjoy the view of this decent man who had come to her aid. Maybe he was worth pursuing, letting in a bit more. He hadn't complained, hadn't been put off by how much of an arse she had been the night before. Instead he had simply loved her. It had been special; realising that now, she felt less angry at the world.

As they closed, Hope saw Allinson approach the second dip. Her eyes then saw something reflect in the falling rays of the sun. It looked long and thin. It came again, glinting very briefly. Like some sort of thin wire, running in a circle around the dip. There was a small metal stake in the ground, hard to see, that the wire passed through before it continued towards another one.

And then Hope's brain understood what she was seeing. And Allinson, only ten feet from her, stepped forward, about to sweep the wire with his foot. She could not stop his action. She yelled and ran forward throwing herself at the officer.

'Allinson!'

As she hit him and they fell, she felt the soil around her erupt violently and a loud noise thundered around her. And then the soil was landing on her back with Allinson underneath her.

Chapter 9

Hope stood at the rear of the ambulance and watched the paramedic attending to Allinson, a large bandage being applied to his arm which had received a deep cut. She had got away lightly, a few scratches here and there, but both had been lucky. If they had been closer, or fallen towards the device, it was likely one or both may not have been able to walk away.

Night had descended and there was a circus around the building. Hope had ordered everyone to stay back until they could get experts on the scene to make sure there were no more explosive devices. The area had been cordoned off as best they could but there was going to be a presence kept to ward off any onlookers. Fortunately, they were quite far away from the main residences on Mull. But as Hope watched the paramedics patch up Allinson, she was approached by a uniformed officer.

'DC McGrath?'

'Yes.'

'There's a woman on the edge of the perimeter looking for 'the boss' as she calls it. I think she knows the owner of the building, at least that's what she says. Do you want to see her, or shall I just get some details given the hour?'

'Show me,' said Hope.

The woman was maybe forty or forty-five, and she had the look of a hard-working soul about her. Although not unattractive, her face had been weathered and she stood with a small stoop. She had curves but also the excesses that came with age, and her hair looked in need of a wash, distressed as it was, black intertwined with a touch of white. She wore a fleece that had seen better days and a pair of wellingtons with jeans.

'Are you the boss?' asked the woman as she saw Hope approach.

'Yes I am. The officer says that you know the householder. Is that correct?'

There was a glint in the eye of the woman as she responded. 'Yes, you could say I know Malkie.'

'And you are, ma'am?'

'Ciara Nixon.' The voice had a harsh tone to it and Hope thought at first it was the west coast of Scotland but further south. Then she recognised the Northern Irish trait of little lip movement as she spoke. 'I live next door, which is a joke as it's nearly a half mile away. But is Malkie all right? I knew he was a rascal behind it all, but this is some serious crap he's in.'

'Come with me,' said Hope and led the woman to her car, offering her the passenger seat. Hope sat in the driver's seat and turned so she was almost lying on the seat to look at the woman.

'Have you been on Mull long?' asked Hope.

'Nearly ten years—left the province when that bastard started hitting me. It was never worth it anyway.' There was just a hint of regret in the statement but Hope decided not to pursue the thought as she had more important things to look into.

'You said you knew Malthe.'

'Malthe? You mean Malkie. I knew he was foreign but he always called himself Malkie. I never did get his surname, not that it mattered.' The woman seemed suddenly down.

'Are you okay?' asked Hope.

'Is he dead?'

'Why do you ask?'

'Well, all this, dear. I mean, look at it. Explosions tonight and then there was that commotion when he went away. I knew something was up. There was this one-armed man who visited him, saw him a couple of times over the last year. I never spoke to the man but I recognised the accent one day when I overheard him talking to Malkie.'

'What was he talking about?' asked Hope.

'Oh, I don't recall, love, but it was an accent from home, close to Belfast but not proper Belfast if you catch my meaning. It was somewhere around there, I'd say—smooth talker though, like he'd polished our rough spots.'

'Did Malkie say who he was?'

'No, dear, you need to understand, I knew Malkie, and he told me things but not things like that. His affairs were private, a no-go area. It was the only time he got angry . . . when I asked about his past and any people he knew. So I didn't.'

'So what sort of a relationship did you and Malkie have?'

The woman crossed herself and then bowed her head for a moment. 'May the good God above forgive but a woman has needs. We were companions; I think that's the word that makes sense. We just kept each other company on nights. He would come round and fix whatever was needing doing in my house and then we'd talk and stay warm by the fire. And we'd also . . . well, you know dear . . . we all have our needs, don't we? It doesn't go away from some of us, and well, he was a man so he had his.'

Hope smiled. She could not understand the woman's embarrassment at this revelation and it did not matter to the investigation. But the commotion she mentioned and this one-armed man did. 'What was all this commotion you talked about?'

'A week ago, he came over to the house with a bottle of red wine. He cooked me dinner, fish, some foreign dish, and then he sits me down by the fire. He told me he had to go, there was going to be trouble but that he'd be back in touch with me but that it could be a while. Then we stayed up all night and well, you know. It was a very sweet night but also a very sad one. I knew I was losing him.'

The woman broke down in tears and Hope let her cry. After a few minutes, she raised her head and looked at Hope. 'You don't always get second chances, and he was mine. So tell me, is he dead?'

Hope nodded and the woman bent over sobbing. She left the woman for a few minutes before asking her further questions. 'Did you see any of the others that caused this commotion?'

'No. He told me to stay clear. For my safety. But when he didn't come over after three days, I went to look and I could tell something was wrong. He always knew when I was coming and he'd come to the door. But the door was ajar. I went inside and saw the mess in the back room. So I just left. But when I saw you people with your lights and that, I thought I might get an answer. Didn't I bloody just.'

'We might need you further, Ciara, to come in and make a statement. But I'll get someone to drive you home and then stay outside; you might be in danger.'

The woman shook her head. 'I'm in no danger—Malkie said so. Said they would want him only. No civilians would be hurt. Said he'd done something terrible and this would be his punishment if it came. But he said I was safe. And he meant it.'

'Maybe so, but I have reason to disagree, so I'll be placing a car outside your house.'

The woman looked almost terrified at the suggestion. 'No, the neighbours will know about me and Malkie. Just send an unmarked one and they can come inside and use the front room. No one knew about Malkie and my relationship with him. No one knew we were special to each other. Malkie was careful of that, and me too, until now. But what's it matter now he's dead?'

The woman began crying again and Hope left the car to organise someone staying with her tonight. Hope felt for the woman and when she said it was all over and saw her loss, something inside clutched at Hope and dug its nails into her. *Not the time, too much to do.* She saw Allinson stepping out of the rear of the ambulance and she wanted to be back in the room in Cromarty, being held for the night. *What happened to me? I used to be strong,* she mused.

'How you feeling, Allinson?' asked Hope.

'Just a few scratches and a bit of a deep cut. But a lot better than I would have been if you hadn't intervened. I owe you one, McGrath. That was a bit too close for my liking.'

'As long as you are all right. I'll ring the boss and give him an update and see what he wants. Personally, as we are waiting for the explosives' guys and forensics, I think we should get some rest and come back in the morning. There won't be much to do before then.'

She left Allinson and returned to the car to make her call.

As she sat with the mobile to her ear, she watched Allinson walking among the other officers and his easy way with them. Everyone seemed to like him, even those that didn't know him. Hope certainly found him an easy blanket to wrap around herself.

'Yes, Hope, tell me it's gone well down your end.' Macleod sounded frustrated.

'Are you okay, sir, you sound a bit shaken?'

'I nearly got my wingman killed today. These people are bit more serious than we are used to. It's not just a case of finding them; they know how to come after you. But how are things on Mull?'

'It's okay, sir.' Hope debated how to put the explosion to Macleod but honesty was usually best. 'We saw the spot where he stole the car from but there's nothing there really. Here on Mull his house was interesting, like someone just passing through, very sparse. But his back room was a mess, a fight and blood spilt on the day he left by the looks of it. Allinson spotted a shed out the back and there were weapons secreted under it. He then spotted two dips that turned out to be hides. One had radio equipment and the other was booby trapped. We nearly lost Allinson but no harm done and the military are on their way. So there might be something more there.'

'Sounds eventful. Everyone okay?'

'Yes, but it was close. I also found his woman down here, a Ciara Nixon. She was enlightening. It seemed he was very discreet and she was his main source of companionship. They were—*Macleod didn't like the term shagging*—intimate. She's pretty cut up about it but she'd no idea where he'd gone. He kept her out of anything he had going on to protect her.'

She heard Macleod sigh down the mobile. 'I hoped you

would have more as we lost our lead up here. Found the Mini and then lost them. They also disposed of the young girl the ferryman got close to. Slit her throat and dumped her at a caravan park. And it was the women in the Mini, I'm sure of that.'

'Well, it was the men down here that chased him out; Ciara says so. She reported seeing Malthe meeting a one-armed man with a Belfast accent, but a softer one.'

'One-armed man?' said Macleod. 'Sounds like it's all going like a TV movie. We need something real we can get our teeth into. At the moment we are chasing ghosts; we need to know what this is about. What's your plans?'

'Bed, sir. It's dark here and we are waiting for the ordnance guys and the forensics before we can get at much else, so I've put some protection on Ciara Nixon, just in case, and I am going to bed somewhere, when I work out where.'

'Okay, Hope, it's your call down there. Just get me something tomorrow. We need something to tag onto.'

'Yes sir.'

Hope switched the call off and sat in the car staring at the dashboard. They were just chasing ghosts at the moment. They didn't even know what this was all about and there were two dead already. She saw Allinson walking over and rolled down her window.

'Allinson, get us a place to stay from the local guys, somewhere decent and I'll make sure everything's set for tonight.'

Hope exited the car and spent a half hour ensuring everything was in order before she sat in the passenger seat as Allinson drove her in the dark. Her brain was muddled now and she needed sleep. When the car rolled up to a small hotel, she laboured with her small bag to the reception and then with her keys to her door.

'Do you want to eat?' asked Allinson. 'You know you really should.'

Hope agreed and after a quick dinner she made for her room. Allinson said he would remain in the bar area to watch some television and she had wished him a pleasant night. After a shower, Hope climbed under her sheets and lay in the dark. Sleep did not arrive and she was soon on her mobile, checking messages and generally doing nothing. And then she felt the cold. It was not real, just an incessant shiver without him beside her.

Hope sniffed and wiped her eyes. *God, I'm pathetic. Come on, girl, just sleep.* After another hour of basically moping, Hope grabbed a t-shirt from her case and threw her jeans on. She walked in her bare feet to the bar and ordered a bottle of red to go. As she waited, she turned and saw Allinson who was now looking at her. She flicked her hair back, mess that it was and then indicated to him a question. Was he coming?

Turning back to the bar, she collected her wine before feeling a hand holding her own. *Yes, everyone liked Allinson, so why not? She needed him, didn't she? I don't care if I'm being weak, I need someone.*

Chapter 10

'Seoras, you need to sleep. Get back to bed.'

Macleod sighed and turned to look at Jane, wrapped up in the duvet, her hair flopping round her neck as she sat up. It had probably been a bad idea to ask her to meet him at the accommodation in Cromarty but he was so tired and he wanted to see her. Not that he had said a lot but at least she knew he wanted her and was not simply running off with the job. She had not complained about that but he was wary of it nonetheless.

'I'm fine. You go back to sleep, I'll be there shortly.'

'You are not fine,' she said. 'You're wound up tight as anything. It's not difficult to see the pressure you're under.'

He watched her throw back the covers and stand up from the bed. She did not even look at him as she covered her body with a t-shirt and then climbed into her jeans.

'Are you going?' he asked.

'Don't be daft, and get some clothes on. We're going to take a walk and calm you down. No point pacing about in here when we can walk this off.'

'It's three in the morning, woman,' protested Macleod.

'I said get changed.' Jane smacked his backside and then disappeared downstairs. When he had changed and followed her down, he found her filling up two cups, the travel mug kind with the screw lids. She had her coat on and his was lying across one of the chairs.

'Come on,' she said.

They completed a circuit of the town before Jane made him sit on a bench by the sea. As he sat drinking his coffee he was aware that he had no conversation, his mind elsewhere. But she simply sat there holding his hand. And then she turned to him.

'Fancy a skinny dip?'

'What?' A knot of fear grew inside him. He had not known Jane that long but she was prone to do the odd crazy thing. It was one of her attractions but sometimes it went past his boundaries.

'Kit off, come on, let's go al fresco.' She had taken her coat off already and was about to take her top off.

'Jane, it's the middle of Cromarty, someone might see.'

'It's the edge of Cromarty, it's four o'clock and the place is dead. Nothing wrong with going for a bit of a swim.' He reached forward as she lifted her top past her belly. Then he caught her eye and began to laugh.

'That's not fair, don't do that to me,' he said.

'You needed picking up and if I had to, you know I would have gone the whole way with this for you.'

'I know. It's just the damn case. We have nothing, just nothing. I'm waiting on leads being followed up, waiting on Hope getting back about things, waiting on this and that. I'm just wound up and frustrated.'

'Well,' said Jane, 'I have a cure for that.'

Macleod went to grab her before she started back on the skinny-dipping notion, but had to halt when he realised she was reaching for her jacket pocket.

'This one was really something, Seoras. I think it's one of three I like. But what do you think?'

Macleod shook his head. 'I can't think at the moment. Sorry.'

'It's a bloody house, Seoras. Snap out of it. It's not your life I'm asking you to sign away. I just want you to look at these pictures and tell me what you think of the damn house.'

Macleod looked at her face. She was angry, but there was also a caring grin behind it. On the force, they would have said she had his back. As he looked at Jane standing in her t-shirt and jeans on a cool morning, he thought of how they always told him to count his blessings at the Sunday school he had attended. Well, maybe he should do just that.

It was six o'clock when he climbed out of bed having returned to it only an hour earlier. The conversation about the house had been quite lively once they had started assigning rooms. And although his body was still tired, his mind was in a better place. He hadn't slept when he had returned to bed, simply holding onto Jane for the hour of rest he was afforded. But it had been better than walking the room, restless.

Jane had dressed and was waiting for him as he was about to depart. With the accommodation being open for whoever needed it, she had decided to return to the hotel. As he closed the door and locked it, he felt her hands run inside his jacket and rummage around his chest. He turned around and they had a moment where he thought they must have looked like teenagers, passionately kissing in total ignorance of the world. Except they looked a lot older and probably less like the movies.

Macleod bounced into the hall where his team were working, the nightshift still there and some of the day shift arriving. DC

Ross waved at him as he entered and pointed to an officer at a desk at the side of the hall. As Macleod approached, the man stood up and Macleod thought he was going to salute.

'It's fine, sit down,' said Macleod and then leaned over the man's shoulder to look at his computer screen. A list of names and dates were on the screen. 'What's this?' asked Macleod.

'Had it back from the Danes early this morning, sir. Malthe Amundsen used to be in their military. Apparently, he was in covert operations but according to the Danes, there's no reason for any comeback from the military operations he was in. They have given us records up until he went into the black ops period when for obvious reasons they don't want to say. But it is a list of his colleagues from the different sections he worked in and some he commanded.'

'Good,' said Macleod, 'now what can we do with this? I suggest you try and see if any of these names are in the UK at present or have visited recently. Unfortunately, we haven't got the later commands so we need to see what the past shows us. Are there any reports on Amundsen there?'

'Some basic stuff, sir, model soldier by the looks of it. But it's all quite sterile.'

'To be expected, but see what you can dig up with it.'

Macleod made his way to his desk on the stage and asked Ross for a brief. The Mini had been dumped a short distance from the site of his incident the previous day and forensics were now examining it. No hospitals had reported any women calling in with appendix issues. Ross continued with some detail about the poison used and how tracing it would be difficult but Macleod had something ticking in his head, ready to spring forward. *Quist!*

'Hold it, Ross,' said Macleod and he strode off the stage and back to the young man he had spoken with previously. 'Is there a Quist on the list?'

'Hold on, sir, I'll just check.'

Macleod felt like he was standing on hot coals as he stepped from one foot to the other. It was unlikely unless the woman who had killed Amundsen were also Danish military. They did not have strong accents—in fact, they sounded more English rather than anything else. But you had to cross check everything; you never knew when you got lucky.

'There's two Quists mentioned, sir. One from the early part of his career, Jonas Quist, and another from the later part, Nils Quist. Their records don't give out details like addresses and movements afterwards. I'll need to call them.'

'Do it,' said Macleod.

It was probably going to take some time contacting the Danish authorities, so Macleod returned to his brief from Ross. Forensics had identified the poison that killed Malthe as Batrachotoxin, the same substance secreted by poison arrow frogs.

'If it gets into your blood stream you will be dead inside of ten minutes,' said Ross. 'It was injected into the bloodstream but we're still unsure exactly how but we know where.'

'Would he have been able to have written anything in those ten minutes, assuming he knew he had been poisoned?' Ross shook his shoulders. 'There's too much that went on that ferry that we don't know about.'

Macleod received a check-in from Hope who was simply stating she was on her way back to Amundsen's house. She sounded brighter and maybe a night's rest had done her some good.

Macleod went back to looking through reports and witness

statements from the local area until the officer contacting the Danish authorities came back to him.

'Sir, I have details on both Quists you asked for. One, the later one, Nils Quist, is still in the military and currently on the south coast of England on exercise. The earlier one, Jonas Quist, left the army some years ago but they believe he came to Scotland and married a woman from here. That's all they have.'

'Quick,' said Macleod, 'the phone book. See if we have any Quists in the north of Scotland. She said he was in the area.' The officer nodded and went back to his desk. He returned a few minutes later.

'Negative, sir. No Quists showing.'

'Try the electoral rolls. Any database lists we have for up here. And actually, try names ending in Quist, double barrelled names. Things like that. Wide as you can with the parameters.'

Macleod sat down and ate his breakfast while he waited. Someone had picked up croissants and bacon rolls from the bakery around the corner and Macleod happily tucked in. No doubt Jane would be sitting at the breakfast table at the hotel. She had a hearty appetite and she was going to be busy again today, as she said she had another six properties to see.

His thoughts were interrupted by the waving hands of the officer he had tasked.

'Sir, I have something. Jones-Quist, living at Ardersier, village beside the airport. Gives a first name of Alison. Nothing else but that. Here's the address.' The officer handed Macleod a piece of paper. Macleod shouted over to Ross who was putting on his jacket in preparation for his return to the accommodation after his nightshift.

'We need the car, Ross. This could be it. Get some uniformed officers to back us up, but we need to do this quietly.'

Within five minutes they were on the road and heading to Ardersier. As the Black Isle countryside shone in the morning light, Macleod marshalled his thoughts about how to approach the building. Last time, he had nearly lost an officer. This time he'd need to be more careful, but this might be their only chance. He felt the adrenalin rising again, that thrill of the chase. He was no longer waiting—he had his target and needed to perform.

Looking at the map function on his mobile, Macleod traced the house to the outskirts of Ardersier, just past the airport. The house had a rear facing the Moray Firth and the village lay on a small piece of land that jutted slightly out to the sea. Looking at the road configuration, Macleod saw he could cut off the village and called the other units to do so. Ross and himself would make an initial call to the house; after all, this could be the wrong person, or possibly just the married spouse.

As they drove up to the house, Ross parked the car at the end of the short driveway. The building had one story and a small garage to the side. Looking deserted in the sunshine that was now breaking through the clouds, it sat aloof from the other buildings separated by a parking space for those who wanted to gaze out to the Firth. It looked deserted in the sunshine that was now breaking through the clouds. Macleod told Ross to wait at the car and he walked along the stony path which crunched under his feet.

The wooden door sat between two large windows and as he passed one, Macleod looked in to see a woman in Lycra performing yoga in front of a television. She could only be mid-twenties and in good shape, her blonde hair running in folds down onto her shoulders. Before he rang the doorbell,

Macleod checked the other window and found an empty room with a small dining table complete with a vase of flowers. So far, so normal.

The doorbell played a tune he could not quite recognise though he knew it would bug his mind in days to come. The door opened promptly and the blonde woman who had been practising yoga now stood before him, obvious sweat marks staining her Lycra outfit. Macleod smiled as she wiped her face with a towel.

'DI Macleod, madam, I was wondering if you had a Jonas Quist living here?'

The woman nodded politely. 'Yes, there is. He's my husband and he's just out the back. Give me a moment.'

Macleod stepped forward. 'If you don't mind, could I accompany yourself to him. It's important.'

'Sure.' She had a soft Welsh lilt in her voice and showed no signs of any hesitation or concern at the request. Macleod wondered if he had the right Quist. The woman led Macleod through to a conservatory at the rear of the house where a man lay sleeping in a chair. He was in his boxer shorts and was bare chested though he had enough hair on his chest to stuff a duvet. A full beard adorned the face and his complexion was distinctly white otherwise.

'Jonas, police. It's a policeman, dear.'

The man opened his eyes slowly and then adjusted himself on the chair. 'I'm sorry, it was a long night.' The accent was strange; a lot of his words were in the local dialect but some came across like they were jutting out like a rocky outcrop, and Macleod could hear the touch of Scandinavian.

'Good morning, sir, are you Jonas Quist?'

'Jonas Quist; yes, I am he, or more accurately I am Jonas

Jones-Quist. Thank you, Gemma. I'll speak with the officer alone.'

Macleod stepped across the door. 'I'd rather you both stayed here.'

'Of course, you are worried that she may run. But you are too late, my friend, they have already gone. And good riddance.'

'How long?'

'Since the early hours of this morning, maybe six. That's why I was sleeping, it was a long night and not one Gemma wants to remember. Please, sir, take a seat, and Gemma will bring us some coffee and I will tell you everything.'

'I'll help her make it,' said Macleod, 'but you stay here. No running off.'

'Run off. Look at me, the neighbours would have a . . . canary, that's how you say it?'

Macleod smiled. Ross would be able to see anyone leave and so he made his way to the kitchen with Gemma Jones and watched her make three cups of coffee.

'Can I ask how you met Jonas?'

'Sure,' she replied as she poured the hot water into a cafetiere. 'I came up here to complete my degree and I was out one night at a gig in Inverness where he chatted me up. He has a real way with words. I took a punt on him and it's paid off. We were married three years ago. I know what you are thinking, he's old enough to be my dad, and that's true. In fact, he's a year older than my dad. But he's been nothing but brilliant to me. Last night was the first time I've ever seen him stressed, and even that he handed brilliantly.'

'In what way?' asked Macleod.

'Well, they came to threaten and force him to do his work but he stayed calm, and he kept me safe, even when they threatened with knives. But she was really in a bad way, and Jonas doesn't like to see anyone ill or injured. He used to be a doctor, a field surgeon. He still has it.'

When the coffee was brought through, Jonas sat up and drank it slowly. 'I guess you want to know everything. I told them you would and I told them I would tell you. But it's things you would have found out anyway. I asked them to not tell me how they came to be in this state and not to say where they were going. I did nothing but heal them, or at least patch her up as best I could.'

Macleod grimaced. He was hoping he might get more but at least he would know who he was looking for. 'So, from the top, who are they and what did you do last night?'

'They are Anna and Freja Fiske. Anna is the mother and also was a colleague of mine in the Danish army. Freja I had never met until last night, but she has the fire her mother has, maybe more so. They came to the door and Anna was in great abdominal pain. She has a burst appendix and I told her to go to a hospital. But she said she couldn't. I asked no more because Freja had a knife, a proper weapon, and she said she knew how to use it. She actually held it to Gemma's throat at first, but I managed to get them to calm down. I did what I could with the equipment I have but it was a patch-up job, a temporary effort like we would have done in the field. She still needs more. A lot more.'

'And you have no idea why they were in such a state?'

'Appendix can go wrong whenever but why they threatened, no. But I was not stupid enough to ask or find out. I had Gemma to keep safe.'

'A wise choice, Mr Quist,' said Macleod. 'And how did they leave?'

'Black Audi. Number plate is written down on the table. But I doubt they will still be in it.'

'I doubt so, too. I think you have both been very lucky. Two days ago, a man was killed on the ferry in Cromarty; you may have seen it on the news. I am pursuing the Fiskes for that murder. The man who died was Malthe Amundsen.'

Quist was visibly shocked. 'No, not Malthe. He was a good man he had tried to help. It was he who had brought me into it.'

'Into what?'

'It was the last night before Malthe and others were shipping out onto active duty with the Danish Military and they were having a party, a final blast you say. I wasn't going with them but was on the base when Malthe brought Anna to me, saying to look after her and keep it quiet. She was a mess and was trembling. Her uniform was in tatters. She told me she had been with three men from the battalion, had been a little drunk, and they had taken advantage.

'You see Anna was quite something back then. Really attractive but also good with people, very friendly and a good soldier, they said. But she was not for having affairs or messing about with any of the men. And some decided that she should be like that. They took her to a private room when she was drunk and I think she endured a hell. From the marks on her body that night and the little that she told me, it was extreme and unpleasant.'

'And did the military authorities do anything about it?'

'No, they never found out about it. Anna told me she did not want anyone to know and she told Malthe to make sure she was able to leave and leave well. Malthe was too kind to her; he should have reported it as the senior officer. But he did as she asked though I don't think he was ever happy about the decision. Anna took up a role in the embassy in the UK as I recall, a security post. Malthe had connections.'

'And the men that did it, got away scot free?' asked Macleod.

'Malthe was angry and he gave them the beating of their lives. But they continued in the army after Malthe went into the special ops. I didn't know he was in Scotland.'

'Do you have the name of the others? They may be at risk.'

'Yes, I can give you the names. Oscar Borgen, Magnus Digman, and Felix Nyman. I treated their wounds after Malthe beat the shit out of them. But if you ask me, officer, you should just let her alone. They deserve what's coming to them. Malthe should never have covered it up, even when she asked. I should not have either, but she was my patient and she asked me to.'

Macleod stood up, having noted the names on his small notepad. 'Do you know where these men went or where they are?'

'No, but she will. Anna was always resourceful, clever. Maybe the military will find them for you. If not, you'll find them dead soon enough. I don't envy you.'

Chapter 11

Hope was bored. This job got like that at times but right now she believed was one of the worst times she had experienced. She was sitting on the bonnet of her car, sipping a coffee, while watching the explosives' experts make the second hide safe. The key thing was to make sure that anything in the hide was not destroyed and with that in mind they were taking their time. A good reason but it was still boring to be waiting for them.

Or maybe she was just restless. Allinson was also drifting about and Hope was finding that difficult. Twice she had taken him to bed for comfort and still she had not spoken to him the following morning in any meaningful way. Either he was a most patient man or he just enjoyed the sex. And maybe that was the real problem she was having. When there was something to do she did not have to think about what she was doing with her life, how she was being an emotional wreck. She was never into casual relationships either and she was having to tell herself Allinson was not a flippant moment. So why did she not speak to him about it?

'Forensics are nearly through with the house and maybe another hour or so with the army ordnance experts.'

She had not seen Allinson approach her but had simply

thought of him in the general vicinity. Now right in front of her, she could only manage a simple 'Thanks.' Maybe she should speak to Macleod about her situation. No, that would not be a good idea. He'd be disgusted by the way she was just jumping into bed with Allinson, just using him as a blanket. Maybe Jane though. She seemed a bit more modern. *God, when did I stop having my own friends?*

It was two hours later when the ordnance team came to her and declared the area safe. They had opened the second hide and inside had found a laptop and several portable hard drives. Hope sent Allinson to the local station with the items and said she would join him shortly, once she had gone through the house with forensics.

The lead investigator for the forensic team was a middle-aged man called Stevens. With a pot belly and a tendency to smoke a pipe, Hope had seen him trundling back and forth from the house to take in the not-so-fresh air several times. He had thick-rimmed glasses and now as he spoke, he did so with a hoarse voice that disguised a raw Yorkshire accent.

'Looking at the blood in the rear room and several markings on the floor and at the front door, I would say that the owner was surprised by someone but gave them a hell of a fight. Someone certainly had their head knocked off the washing machine door. We have various samples of blood, clothing, and flesh which I'll get to the lab and see if we can get a match for. Mackintosh should be able to give me DNA from our victim and I'll see if she has any other from the car. We might get a match but I guess you're thinking these are the same people. I mean how many people can be after someone. Especially out here.'

As it was daylight, Hope took another walk through the

house to see if she missed anything in the dark. It was unlikely and forensics had also been over the entire house, so she was not expecting anything new. But as she walked around she found herself distracted. This was a delaying tactic, avoiding Allinson. There was nothing else to learn here.

After speaking to the sergeant on scene about what level of security the house required when all the teams had left, Hope took her car and started the drive to Tobermory and the main police station. On the way, she spied a small cafe and pulled over. Breakfast had not happened that morning, indeed she had barely managed a shower before they left. Bed had seemed too good to leave. Or rather Allinson had.

Hope was in the middle of her scrambled eggs when she got the call from Macleod. He updated her on his trip to Ardersier and how he believed they were now looking at a revenge killing, and possibly more to come.

'One thing I don't understand, Seoras,' said Hope, 'who is looking for who? If both sets of people were there to kill Malthe, the soldiers and Anna Fiske, would they both not be looking for the other? And who is Fiske's partner in all this? You don't just jump on board a killing spree; you tend to need something to bring you on board.'

'Agreed,' said Macleod. 'And, also, why now? Whatever they did to her, and Quist said it was horrible though he did not know all the details, it was definitely sexually abusive in nature. Why did she not react earlier? It seems a long time. And why Malthe? I mean, why him first? Of all the players, he seemed to have been the most decent; after all, he did what she asked and then helped her out, before giving the soldiers a beating for doing it.'

'We're missing something, Seoras.' There was silence on the

other end of the mobile phone and Hope continued to eat her eggs.

'See if the laptop gives you any further information, Hope. You said Malthe had a woman down there. Any chance he could have given her something to keep safe?'

'She never mentioned anything but it's possible.'

'She might not even know she's got it,' said Macleod. 'Given how brutal these parties are I would suspect he wouldn't tell her, just come back to her if he's alive and then pick up what he had hidden.'

'I'll check with her again. I put an officer on her house last night, and I'll keep one there. Plain clothes job though; I don't want to attract attention if they don't know about her already.'

'Good,' said Macleod. 'Talk to me once you have anything on the laptop. We're still tracing the hospitals as she can't be in a good way, even after Quist's help. I've got the team working with the embassy in London, trying to follow her route in the UK, see if we can find her home. We're also trying to find the soldiers through the Danish army, see where they are now. Now we have names it might be easier.'

Hope finished off her breakfast before driving to the north of the Isle of Mull and to the station in Tobermory. The picturesque port was shining in a warm light when she got there and found the small police station. Allinson was in a room on his own, working with the laptop, trying to break in.

'Hi,' he said on her arrival. 'I have a little expertise in these sorts of things, but I'm also on the line to Glasgow to see if we can't break into the data.'

'The DI's found some more detail on everyone. I'll update you when you have a moment. Stick with the laptop at the moment though. It could be our best lead.'

'Will do, McGrath. You okay?'

'Of course,' said Hope and turned away from him. 'Why wouldn't I be?'

'If that's how you want it, fine. But if you want more than company, let me know.'

'I don't know what you mean,' lied Hope. But Allinson had his head buried in his work, and in fairness, that was the response her lie had deserved.

Hope was at a loose end, waiting for the laptop to reveal its secrets and she took a walk along the bay at Tobermory. The houses were a multitude of colours and she saw tourist shops and cafes and a chip shop as she walked. The harbour had an orange lifeboat berthed and she saw the coastguard station close by. Even this *populated* part of Mull was quiet and she understood why Malthe had come here if he wanted to be away from the world.

Her unfairness to Allinson was bugging her but she decided to block out those thoughts by dwelling on the issue in hand. *What would drive me to hunt and kill someone? If they had abused me, why not do it? Fiske has had army training so she can handle herself but then she waits for years before coming after them. And who is her partner? She's younger, much younger.*

Hope sat down at a coffee house, ordered a drink, and watched a woman walking along the sea front with a pram before her. The woman stopped and picked up the child hugging it tightly before pointing out the boats in the bay to it. The child was a young baby less than a year old, maybe. Hope caught the woman's eye and she came over smiling.

'He's very cute,' said Hope, thinking this was a generous comment to make.

'Thank you, she is. They have a way of getting hold of you.

Do you have any of your own?' Hope shook her head. 'Still, plenty of time to have your own.' The woman suddenly went silent before she mumbled, 'If you want any, of course. Sorry, I hope you don't have any issues.' The woman's face was now red. 'I mean, God, I'm making such a mess of this; if you want or can have any, if there's no reason you can't, there's clearly still time.'

Hope watched the woman turn away in horror at her own babble. 'It's okay; please have a seat—she's lovely. I don't have any children because I haven't wanted any.'

'Thank God,' said the woman a little too strongly. 'I had to wait years for this wee one. We had a few issues and that but we got there. Once they get under your skin, they just grab you; you'd do anything for them.'

Hope smiled but inside an idea was trying to surface. As the woman continued to talk, she smiled and did not listen to one word. Five minutes later, the woman moved on, pushing the pram and Hope watched her go before pulling out her mobile.

'Macleod.'

'Seoras, did Quist say anything about what happened from the sexual abuse—what results there were?'

'No,' said Macleod, 'not sure what you mean.'

'Kids, Seoras, did she have any children? Ask the embassy. I guess Malthe may have known as he looked after her. Maybe the missing link is a kid. After all, she wouldn't be the first parent to kill for a kid.'

'But why now?' asked Macleod.

'I don't know, just a hunch. It just seems that everything was dealt with as she wanted and then she suddenly changes.'

'But the kid would be early twenties, wouldn't they?'

'I know. So, what's happened to cause this? Maybe that's her kid with her.'

A few moments later the conversation closed, Macleod telling Hope it was just a hunch and that's how it should be treated until there was more evidence. But Hope was feeling positive about the idea. *This was a woman stirred to kill. There must be a kid. And I'm going to bloody find her.*

Chapter 12

I t was with renewed zeal that Hope walked back to the Tobermory police station and when her mobile buzzed as she was only a few hundred metres from it, with the legend 'Allinson' appearing on the screen, she got even more excited. When she entered the room he was working in, his smile could have lit up the room on its own.

'I'm in. But there's a lot of files to work through. It looks like he was trying to trace someone. From a very brief scan, and I do mean very brief, Malthe was looking at things from the Danish Embassy to child adoption papers to newspaper reports. Looks like it goes across about twenty years at least.'

'Twenty years,' repeated Hope excitedly. *Maybe I'm right.* 'We need to break this search down and get it all over to the DI as well. Can you print off copies of everything here so we can look through them? I'll ring the boss.'

Hope stepped outside and advised Macleod what detail was coming his way. She tried as best she could to not drive her *daughter* theory at Macleod again but it was hanging on the edge of her words. When she was done, she came back inside, took Allinson's coffee order, and went off to find a shop while the printing took place. On return, she found some empty cardboard files and began to take the printed material to place it in the correct folder. Then she sat down and with a highlighting pen began to look over the documentation.

The station was not large and the room they were sitting in had one table and little else in it. But Hope and Allinson spent the day there, only surfacing for dinner. Hope always found that it was best to step back at some point and digest what was being looked at. They found a small pub and ordered fish and chips, before sitting at a bay window overlooking the water. The waitress brought their meals and stood looking out of the window commenting on how lovely it looked, and how it was always a smart place for couples.

'Err . . . we're not together,' said Allinson.

When the waitresses had left, Hope stared at Allinson. 'You didn't have to say that.'

'What should I have said? I've been invited in close to this woman opposite me, properly close, but there's nothing going on. She just uses my arms, enjoys the sex, and then doesn't talk to me. I thought we're not together was a better way to put it.'

'There's no need to be so harsh,' said Hope. But Allinson did not have a look of anger on his face. All she saw was frustration.

'I'm not being harsh. I just don't know if I'm being taken along for a short ride as a comfort blanket or if you're genuinely interested. If I'm just a blanket, then fine, but let me know.'

Confident, killer-catching Hope faded away. The newly dumped Glasgow girl came to the fore and she saw her new rock, albeit an anchorage she was unsure of, falling away.

'Allinson, don't move away. I need you at the moment, I don't know what's happening with me. I don't know. I have this case and I just get immersed in it to push away the other shit. But I don't want you to back away. He left me; please don't do that.'

'So there was someone. At least that makes sense. I'm a rebound, a stop gap.'

'No,' said Hope desperately. 'You're more than that.'

'How? You've never even asked my first name.'

The dinner continued in silence and Hope knew she'd been rightly accused. She found it hard to raise her face and even look at Allinson such was her shame. But as the bill came over she plucked up her courage and grabbed his hand.

'What is it? What's your name?'

'Jonathan, Hope. But you can call me Jon if you want to.'

'Thank you. And I'm sorry. But stick with me, please. I really need you.'

'Me, or just someone.'

Hope nearly blurted out the standard answer but then she stopped herself. He deserved the truth. 'Someone. But I really like you. I'll tell you it all next time.'

'When you're ready, Hope.'

They walked along the seafront and stopped at a bench overlooking the bay. There was no one around and so Hope decided to pull together what they had read that afternoon.

'We know Malthe was looking at records from the Danish Embassy, relating to Anna Fiske's deployment and then subsequent departure. There's no mention of why except it was a mutual decision. It comes three years after she started working for them. And then there's an adoption paper of a family in Kent, of a girl. But there's little else beyond that about them except an address. Then we have various homes and foster parents in England. And then we have the newspaper cuttings.'

'All around human trafficking and slavery,' said Allinson. 'But there's no names. But then the scanned note that was hand written with four names on it, Borgen, Digman, Smith, and Houston. There're some coded letters from Smith and Houston. And that's all. But there's mention of a Houston in a newspaper article, arrested two years ago. And there's a single photo highlighted out from a pack of photos.'

'Lots of naked photos of young women and he has one singled out. Now Malthe seemed to have a stable relationship and so this was part of his investigation, I believe. But it doesn't say who she is. The email with the photos—it had a name with it, didn't it?'

'Maltman,' replied Allinson.

'I'm going back to Ciara Nixon,' said Hope, 'to see if she can add anything further to all this. Get on to Trafficking and see if these names ring a bell. Cross reference and see if they come up anywhere. Especially Maltman—if he's been arrested, he could be a good start.'

'You checking in with the boss or do you want me to do that?' asked Allinson.

'I'll brief him on the way down. I want to follow up on that address for the adoptive parents in Kent. It might give us a good idea what really happened to Fiske all those years ago. She wanted Malthe dead but it took twenty years, so what really happened? And why this trafficking detail with all these girls? Was Freja Fiske trafficked? Ask Macleod if that's her in the picture, but I doubt it as he has not rung already.'

'Will do,' said Allinson, standing up and starting to make his way to the station.

'And Jon, I might be late but wait up. I will tell you a bit more tonight, about why I'm being a colossal shit.'

She watched him smile and Hope felt the surging heroine coming back. Walking to the car, there was a spring in her step and she was already wishing she was on her way back from the far end of Mull.

The drive down to the southern end of Mull took over an hour but Hope was delighted to find Ciara Nixon was at home. The on-duty policeman opened the door and then slunk down to a secreted seat where he could see the road outside. Ciara Nixon was in the kitchen and Hope surprised her.

'Sorry, love, I didn't hear you come in. I was just going to go to bed; it's been a long day.'

The woman's eyes were dark from crying and her hair was a mess. She wore a scarlet dressing gown and Hope was not sure that there was anything else underneath. Although she looked a mess, she did smell good, a touch of jasmine possibly in the air. Ciara took a half empty bottle of whisky and poured herself a large tumbler of it before offering the bottle to Hope.

'No, I'm on duty; otherwise, I might join you.'

'That bad as well? What the hell could a good-looking girl like you have to be sad about?'

'Long story,' said Hope, and it was one she was not going into. 'I've been looking through some papers I found of Malthe's and I want to run some names past you.'

'Sure, but I told you he didn't speak to me about his business. Wanted me kept out of it, said it was too dangerous. Turns out he was right.'

Hope thought the woman was going to burst into tears but instead she downed the contents of the tumbler and poured another. Hope would need to get her to think about these names fast or she would be too drunk to be any use.

'Did you ever hear the name Maltman?' Ciara Nixon shook her head. 'Houston?' Again, a shake of the head. 'Borgen, Digman, Nyman?' No recognition. 'Fiske?' Again nothing.

Then she had an idea. 'I'm going to show you a picture; Ciara, don't be shocked by it. I want to know if you have seen the girl in the picture, okay?' Ciara nodded and Hope held up a print out of the photograph of the naked girl that had been highlighted above the other photographs of other girls.

'Yes, I've seen that. Men! I found him looking at that and other photographs one day. He made me promise not to talk about it, but now he's dead what's the harm? I thought he was just being lonely, after all, I don't look like that, do I? He had them all spread out in front of him. I gave him hell for it but he kept saying it wasn't what I thought. Still, I forgave him; after all, it was his only fault—he was very good to me.'

'He wasn't being a pervert, Ciara. He was genuinely investigating, or so I believe. Did he say who she was?'

'Only that she was a very special girl. That made me angry, I was his special one. I was . . . ' Ciara broke down and began crying. Hope wandered the kitchen waiting for the woman to sort herself but she was a mix of grief and booze.

'Did Malthe travel a lot?'

'Yes,' sniffed Ciara, 'I know he went to England on business but that was all he would say to me. He never said where exactly or what about. But he was always back fairly promptly.'

'Okay, is there anything else that's come to mind that might help us?' Hope was throwing this in as a chance comment, not expecting much. It was just a way to close the conversation and she would soon thank her.

'Well, there was one thing but it's stupid. On one of his trips he asked me what you would get a man as a gift, something special but practical. I was rabbiting through lots of items, cufflinks, gloves, shirts, other tops and that. He suddenly got frustrated with me and turned around to say the man had only one arm. One pissing arm. I had laughed. Seems silly now but I laughed. They'd lock me up for that these days. Probably discrimination.'

Ciara's head began to fall onto the table, slowly and gently. Soon the woman had fallen asleep. Making her way to the front door, Hope told the officer in the chair the situation and bade him a goodnight.

As she drove back through Mull along roads that swept by the sea and then beside tree-filled hills that gave a silhouette to the clear night sky, she mused on what Ciara had said. A one-armed man—it seemed ludicrous. But then she thought about the need Malthe might have had for a second investigator and that did not seem a silly premise.

As she pulled up to the police station, Allinson was standing outside waiting for her. He jumped into the car and she drove off to the hotel they were staying at.

'How did it go?' he asked.

'Well, that photo is definitely part of the investigation but otherwise she knew little other than he travelled a lot to England. She also muttered about a one-armed man being part of Malthe's investigation team, or certainly involved with him.'

'Sounds a bit Hollywood.'

'I know, but how did you get on?'

'Maltman is a good link and we're on the move tomorrow. Macleod wants us in England to go and see this guy. He's in prison but he's in the middle of bargaining. And he's also said we can drop down to Kent too, if you think it's worth it.'

Hope grinned. Macleod was following her line of enquiry now. She knew he'd come round. 'I'd better get prepped then for that interview, run through some more of those documents to see if there's anything else.'

'No, I've been through them, Hope, and you need a good night's sleep; it'll be a busy day. Are you okay on your own tonight? I think we could both do with a rest, not a competitive, or a deep revelation, night.'

'Sure,' said Hope but she felt exactly the opposite.

After a shower, Hope lay on her bed, looking around her room. She knew she should sleep but her mind kept going back to dinner and what Allinson had said. She had given him nothing, and just taken from him. What did she really want from him? Deep down she knew.

Getting up, she donned her dressing gown and opened her door, walking across the hall to Allinson's room. She knocked lightly.

'Wait a minute.' The door opened a few moments later. 'Hell, Hope, it's two in the morning; what's the crisis?'

'I am.' She stepped inside and shut the door behind her.

Chapter 13

Macleod was sitting at his desk in the hall at Cromarty when his telephone rang. Before him the room was a quiet hub of information gathering, calls being made to the Danish army, embassy, adoption societies, and government departments. It was long, arduous, and very dull. Macleod tried to keep an overview and after all he had learnt from Hope that morning before she began her travels to England, he was more positive they would get a significant breakthrough in the day ahead. But after the visit to Quist, the women seemed to have gone to ground.

The men on the ferry had been another matter. It took a while and some high-level calls to get the full details released from the military about Borgen, Digman, and Nyman. As soldiers, they had been far from the model the Danish army would have wanted but neither did they have anything criminal on their records. Their movements after their departure from the military were not known and they seemed to have left the country several years after Anna Fiske had departed. The details of her departure from the army were sparse but it was by mutual consent and nothing about any incident involving the three men was recorded.

'Macleod.' It had taken him six rings on the telephone before he had answered as he was feeling parched and had a sip at his coffee first. There just seemed to be no rush about the day.

'Are you the fella in charge of looking into the ferry murder?' The voice was calm and smooth but it had a distinct Northern Irish brogue that snapped Macleod's mind to attention.

'Yes. To whom are I speaking?'

'A friend. It's Macleod, isn't it?'

'Detective Inspector Macleod, yes. What can I do for you?' Macleod was frantically waving his arms trying to get someone else to monitor the call.

'More what I can do for you, Inspector. Are you aware of a stopping place south of Aviemore, a place called Ralia? It's near Newtonmore.'

Macleod knew the place well, after all, he had travelled past it many times when coming north from Glasgow to Inverness. As he remembered, it had decent coffee. 'Yes, I know it.'

'Meet me there in two hours and come on your own.'

'Why? Why should I come on my own to meet a man I don't know?'

'Ring Mackintosh. I believe she's your forensic investigator on this case. Tell her you're meeting Smythe. She'll validate my credentials. I believe you can help my client.'

Macleod felt off balance. This man seemed to know a lot and Macleod knew nothing about him. But if Mackintosh could vouch for him, then maybe it was worth following up. He'd set a time anyway then decide if he should go.

'It'll take me a while to get there. I'll be there in two hours.'

'That's perfect. Warn the Inverness force that you will need some backup later today towards evening. Probably eight or so officers to help with the arrest.'

'What arrest?' asked Macleod.

'Ralia, two hours, Inspector. Don't be late.'

The phone went down and Macleod called over an officer and then sent him away. It would be unlikely that the man would leave his mobile number, this would be a one-off call from a free sim card or something similar. He picked up his telephone and called the forensic laboratory. After clearing the receptionist, he heard Mackintosh answer the telephone.

'Detective Inspector, how can I help? I'm afraid we haven't anything else for you here.'

'Smythe. Can you tell me who Smythe is?' Macleod could hear a sharp intake of breath.

'Smythe called you? About the case?'

'Yes, he called me, Mackintosh. Who is he? And why's he so covert?' Macleod was becoming impatient.

'I've met Smythe a couple of times on my travels. He's no time waster, Macleod. If he's asking for you, it'll be relevant and maybe even something important.'

'He's asking for officers as backup.'

Mackintosh gasped over the telephone and Macleod found himself becoming frustrated at the lack of information rolling towards him. 'Just tell me who he is, where he lives, what he's doing in my case.'

'Okay, Inspector, take it easy. He's just a bit of an old flame. I didn't think I'd hear about him again. He was in the force but in Northern Ireland. He lost his arm in an explosion back in the day and left when he was being confined to a desk. He's very determined and sometimes bloody minded. He works in the shadows, you might say, not for anyone in particular but he takes on clients who need help. He never advertises, strictly word of mouth.'

'And is he reliable?' asked Macleod.

'As a partner, no.' Again, there was a deep sigh. 'As a source of information, completely. I'd trust my life on his word. Go see him, Detective Inspector.'

Macleod shifted in his seat. It was quite a recommendation, especially from Mackintosh who Macleod saw as a little frosty and someone who would not trust easily. 'What's he look like?'

'Left arm missing, with an Ulster accent. I'm sure your detective skills can manage that.' Macleod had offended Mackintosh on their first meeting and although they were cordial when working, he felt she was always looking for a little payback. And this sounded like that. He let it slide; after all, she'd been very forthcoming.

'Thank you for that,' said Macleod, 'and thanks for everything on this case. I hope we're on a better footing than we started on.'

'That's pretty big of you, Macleod. We're good, but go meet Smythe. Trust me—it'll be worth it.'

Macleod hung up the telephone and found Ross. Having briefed him about the call, he instructed him to call Inverness about the potential for back up this evening and to await Macleod's check-in with details. He grabbed a couple of croissants from a table of food in the hall, poured himself a coffee in a take-away cup, and then made for his car.

The drive to Ralia was a pleasant one, the car flanked on both sides by mountain or tree-lined verges. As he had climbed up out of Inverness, he had seen a long view of the Moray Firth in the sunshine, stretching out to the east, like it came pouring out from the city, feeding under the Kessock Bridge, the picturesque structure that sat imposingly between the Black Isle and Inverness.

By the time he had passed Aviemore, he was truly surrounded by mountains and he thought of his drive up with Jane a week previous when they had stopped by the river running alongside the road. The sun had been shining and although it was chilly, it was also so crisp and clean. When the road had quietened for a moment he thought he could stand amongst that beauty forever. Maybe that's what this house hunting was really about. The Isle of Lewis had been his home but he was not looking for a return to island life, rather the balm of solitude among the mountains and valleys.

He swung the car off the road onto the connecting track that led to the car park at Ralia. There was small cafe in a round building that had toilets beneath it, a common resting place from travels on the A9. There were some walks nearby that could refresh your legs after a long drive, and with the grass areas beside the car parks, both children and dogs could be exercised.

The car park was half-full as he drove into a space that sat clear of any other cars by two spaces. From his car, he looked around and could not see anyone with a single arm. He waited five minutes for someone to show but no one came. After his journey, Macleod was needing the toilet and so walked to the facilities at the bottom of the building.

As he stood at a urinal, Macleod heard the door open and then a harsh Ulster accent said, 'This is not the most salubrious place for a chat, Macleod. What would people say, meeting in the gents? I'll be upstairs in the cafe. I hope a latte's good for you.'

The door closed again and Macleod felt just a touch uneasy. How had he missed a one-armed man? But he finished up, washed his hands, and then made his way up the curling stairs of the building to the cafe at the top. The round room had a circular core so that you could not see the whole room at once but had to walk around it for full observation.

There was no single-armed man so Macleod decided to simply sit down near the door. After all, he could maybe see him come in. But then he watched a man at the till pick up a coffee in his right hand and transport it to a window seat. He then returned for another cup and carried it, again in his right hand to the table. The man had a left arm that ended in a glove but it did not seem to move much. The man showed no sign of looking around but instead looked out the window, his coffee before him and one opposite, as if waiting for someone.

Macleod got up and walked over to the man, sitting down opposite. The man turned and smiled. He was of a fairly lean build with neatly cut black hair. His eyes were penetrating and he had not shaved for a day or two, the stumble threatening to run riot if not checked soon.

'Good, you're not one of these thick-as-shit Inspectors, Macleod. I wear the prosthetic in public quite often.'

'Less conspicuous,' said Macleod, 'being a one-armed man makes you stand out. Two arms provide cover, Mr Smythe.' Macleod stared at the man sizing him up but the target of his stare did not flinch.'

'Thank you for coming out here, Inspector, or can I call you Seoras, so we don't attract any undue attention with formalities. Lovely woman you have by the way.'

Macleod started. 'What were you . . .'

'Easy. I was simply finding you because I knew we would need to speak. I doubt she'll remember me but she was very pleasant, helpful to a man looking for directions. I was going to meet you at your hotel you see but then this came up and I need your help.' Smythe sipped his coffee and then looked out of the window. He seemed to be hunting for something in the car park, but his eyes did not rest anywhere and so Macleod thought whatever it was had not arrived.

'Patrick Smythe, by the way, Seoras, but call me Paddy. Formerly of the force, Northern Ireland branch so to speak, but forcibly retired. Also, an employee of Malthe Amundsen. I thought that would grab your attention,' said Smythe as Macleod's face flickered.

'Tell me more,' said Macleod.

'Malthe wanted me to hunt down three men he had worked with in the Danish army; I think you know these men. They were on the ferry when he was killed—that I have since discovered but he wanted me to trace them. Unfortunately, I haven't achieved that objective; I just know where they have been.'

'And where is that?'

'Been involved with a man called Houston. Nasty piece of work. Takes young women, sometimes young girls, kids some of them, and traffics them round the country, sometimes out to Europe. He doesn't care, just moves the stock around for men who have an interest in that kind of thing.'

'Forced prostitution?'

'Exactly,' said Smythe. 'Now I wanted to know why Malthe was looking for them. He didn't tell me, but then not all clients do, so I found out. It helps to know who you're working for, Seoras. I don't like to work for the dark side; I'm still one of the force at heart.' There came a smile with this statement that Macleod found himself warming to.

'Malthe's past,' continued Smythe, 'is shrouded but he had a child, though I don't know where from, called Liva, Liva Amundsen. But she was in foster care. I haven't traced her origins or how she got into care but she was in and out of foster homes. And then she disappeared. I think she's in the prostitution ring. That's why he wants me to find this Houston guy.'

'And you brought me here because? You couldn't just ring me and tell me this.'

'No, I couldn't,' said Smythe, 'because if you look over there at the blue minivan that has just driven into the car park, you will see the driver get out.'

Macleod watched a bald-headed man leave and go over to a car where he climbed inside. Two minutes later, he got out and got back into the minivan. The van did not move but the driver of the car emerged and came towards the building.

Macleod looked questioningly at Smythe but he held up a finger, indicating that Macleod should wait. The driver then appeared at the cafe counter where he ordered take-away coffee before returning to the vehicle. The car drove off, shortly followed by the minivan.

'Shall we go?' asked Smythe. Macleod looked at the Ulsterman for answers. 'That, my dear inspector, was Houston, and that van is full of some of those unfortunate women.'

Chapter 14

'Well, it's entirely your choice, Inspector, but I thought you would want to follow the van and then bring in everyone associated with the operation rather than Houston and this driver. I understand you are following a different case but I'm sure those who work the trafficking back at the station would be grateful to grab as many of them as they could.'

Macleod had to agree. Here was the potential to get into a large operation of people trafficking as well as his case. If he brought the word down then he should be able to get a first crack at Houston, or be in the room.

'I agree with you, Smythe, but I could do with grabbing him now for my investigation. But yes, I have nothing to compel him to talk, and he could just stay quiet and then I'd have to let him go. Being able to arrest him may put some pressure on him to talk.'

'There's the van. I doubt the car will be far away,' said Smythe. Macleod was holding his vehicle several cars back on a busy A9 towards Inverness. He had called ahead to warn the station of the identity of both vehicles and to have unmarked cars ready to track them, in case they managed to lose him.

Smythe was sitting in the passenger seat and had a small

case on his lap from which he had produced some papers and a calculator. Behind his ear was a pencil and he wore a pair of glasses. When Macleod had asked what he was doing, Smythe simply said that no one ever suspected an accountant. Macleod had to agree it was a good idea as two men, one in a suit could look like a police tail, and a bad one at that.

As they approached the outskirts of Inverness, Macleod could see that impressive firth and the Kessock Bridge again, this time before his eyes instead of gawping in the mirror. The sun was shining and the world looked ready for the tourists.

'I wonder how many girls are in the van,' said Macleod.

'Twelve,' said Smythe quietly.

'How do you know that? This wasn't a tip you got, was it?'

'No. It's been three weeks of work, Inspector, so if you could kindly make sure your guys don't balls it up, I would be very appreciative.' There was no anger in the statement, just someone giving a matter of fact feeling.

'Is that a large movement for trafficking?'

'I wouldn't know,' said Smythe. 'I was after Houston, not the girls; their release is just a method of getting to him for my client. Although, I don't mind helping free them at all. Sick, dirty bastards, these guys. I don't hold with anyone being enslaved, Inspector. They deserve gutting but I'm sure they'll get better in our prison system.'

Macleod gave Smythe a hard look. 'This will be by the book. I don't want any freelancing.'

'I said they deserved gutting. I didn't say I had a knife for the job. Don't question my morals here, Inspector. I was on the frontline like you. I know my mind.'

The conversation died as they drove across the Kessock Bridge, with both the car and minivan now in sight. As they cleared the bridge, the van pulled into a resting spot while the car continued. Seeing one of his unmarked cars ahead of him and behind Houston's car, Macleod pulled into the rest area and parked a little distance from the van. The bald-headed man got out and walked over to a pastry shop.

'Go and buy something from there,' said Smythe.

'To keep up the look?' asked Macleod.

'If you like, but I'm bloody starving. Steak slice if they have it. A wee coffee too, Inspector. I'm sure you get expenses for this sort of thing.' Smythe smiled before looking down into his sheets again. With a shrug, Macleod made his way to the pastry counter and stood two persons behind the van driver. The man's voice when he ordered came with a European accent. Macleod could not place it but he would have said Eastern Europe.

Having purchased two steak slices, the hunger pangs beginning to attack his own stomach, Macleod walked back to his car to find it empty. Looking around, he spotted Smythe at a vantage point looking out into the Moray Firth where it passed between Inverness past the old ferry crossing from Kessock.

'Ah, good man yourself, Inspector. The only problem up here is you don't get a wee soda in these establishments. Back home you'd get a wee egg and sausage in a soda farl, dash of the old brown sauce, and the egg running all over the insides. It's belting, Seoras.'

Macleod raised his eyes at the use of 'Seoras'.

'What else would I call you?' said Smythe quietly. 'Can hardly drop the I-word out here in the open. Lighten up, man.'

Smythe pointed out into the Firth. He had a steak slice in his hand as he pointed but Macleod was still holding Smythe's coffee, as well as his own and his steak slice, meaning he had touched neither.

'Have you ever seen the dolphins round here?'

'A few times,' said Macleod. 'They can be quite delightful.'

'I sometimes get them round my boat. Magnificent creatures but they can throw the porpoises about. End up killing them sometimes. They're not sure why but they reckon it might be for fun. You get a lot of that in this game, don't you? Beauty and evil together. When people are wounded it happens sometimes. But sometimes it's just there in them and you can't get it clear. Not easily.'

'No,' said Macleod. He wondered where this ramble in morality was going and he hoped the man would not start on a religious bent. His own days of Presbyterian hardliner thought had disappeared and he saw God differently, less black and white and more mysterious. The daft thing was, it actually made it harder, not easier as they had always said in his first church.

'I heard about the incident up at Embo, Seoras, and then at the train tracks. Be very careful with this bunch you're looking at. Evil and beauty, remember that.'

Macleod said nothing, a little put out by this youngster giving him tips. Smythe could only be about forty at most. But he wasn't for engaging any further for he did not know the man and he was unsure of his motives.

'On the move, Seoras,' said Smythe and Macleod kept his head staring at the sea.

'Tell me when they're gone.'

A few moments later, Smythe gave the nod and they jumped into the car and followed the van out onto the A9. They nearly missed the vehicle as it peeled off and then went under the road to take a back road out onto the Black Isle. They did not travel far before spotting the vehicle parked up at a large farmhouse, flanked by forest on one side and a field on the other. Macleod drove along the road that went through the forest and pulled over at a convenient track. He texted a go signal with his mobile for the backup to get into place around the farmhouse.

This was to be an operation run by the trafficking team and Macleod was to remain on the perimeter with Smythe, who as a civilian was not to be involved. The Ulsterman seemed quite happy at this and walked closer with Macleod until the farmhouse was in view between the trees.

'You can go closer if you want,' said Smythe, 'I won't move, you can trust me. I know how the involvement of anyone outside can screw up these operations. Besides I don't want to be seen; it wrecks the undercover stuff you see.'

Macleod did not trust the man to stay in position and so decided to remain with him as well. This was one for others to execute and then he would have his time in the interview room with Houston. But it made him uneasy, as things can often go wrong in the field and this was by no means a foregone conclusion.

If you looked closely, you could make out the officers moving in around the building. Macleod had already identified the two suspects he knew and the car had been tailed to the farmhouse and Houston identified to the other officers when he stepped out of the car. The key point was to secure the girls.

'Do you know how they run these operations?' asked Smythe.

'Well, it's a standard police operation in that—'

'No, no, no,' said Smythe. 'I mean the traffickers, how they run their business, somewhere like this. The last thing they need is people coming to the place they have the girls. Too many been caught that way with undercover moves and that. Some are now having a place that's a little away from the main building, a place where they can have the girls work without exposing the whole house. Just wondering if they had one here.'

'Well, I can't see anything.'

'We're a bit close, if you ask me. Would be further out. The last one was.'

'Did you catch someone there?' asked Macleod.

'Yeah, caught. Something like that. But the girl got to a refuge; that was the important point.'

Macleod did not know if he wanted to ask more and with the job in front of him he had enough on his plate without investigating the extremely helpful Mr Smythe. He was probably just messing with him, as he had played the upper hand since the meeting at Ralia.

There was a flash of colour amongst the trees and Macleod saw that the operation was in progress. There was quiet for two minutes and then it sounded like all hell had broken in the farmhouse. Women shrieked and officers barked at people to lie down. Everything seemed to be going well and Macleod was relishing his chance in the interview room. As the action seemed to be simmering down, Ross called on his mobile.

'Has it all gone well, sir?'

'It seems to have,' said Macleod, keeping his voice low. 'I should be over at the interview room in the next couple of hours. Anything new at your end?'

'Just to let you know that DC McGrath and DC Allinson are down in England and ready to start tomorrow morning. She said she would touch base with you tonight again.'

'Okay, Ross, that all sounds . . . '

'Over there,' interrupted Smythe, 'in the woods and running. That's Houston!'

Macleod did not hesitate and driving his mobile into his pocket he took off at a pace. The ground was uneven with trees all around and he had to constantly lift his feet which slowed him down. But he had Houston within sight, although the man was ducking in and out of trees along a path that seemed to be better than the one Macleod was taking.

Aware that there was no other pursuit with him, Macleod could only guess that Houston had overpowered someone or managed to come out of a secret passage or door. What had happened was irrelevant anyway, all that mattered was he was on the run and Macleod had to grab him before he was lost to the case. Macleod must have been running a good five minutes when the land began to dip down to the sea and he had to stop and catch breath. But he saw Houston run into a small house that was right on the coastline. There was a car outside, a rather expensive one if Macleod was any judge.

As he made his way down the slope, Macleod could hear a commotion from inside. He ran to the front door which was open and hurtled into a hallway with two doors off of it. He threw open the first one and saw Houston engaged with a man. The man was naked and shouting at Houston who had a knife in his hand. The naked man stared at Macleod in horror but Houston had his back to the Inspector. Instead Houston lashed forward at the man cutting his throat. Macleod saw the neck become red and the man gurgled.

But Houston had turned around and now came at Macleod with the knife. Reaching out with his hands, Macleod grabbed a descending arm with the knife trying to push it back.

Houston was strong and pushed Macleod back into the wall in the hallway where the Inspector's head smacked off the plasterboard and Macleod reeled. Houston took the knife back but a hand grabbed his arm. He struggled with it, a pale white arm that belonged to a brown-haired woman in a sheer dressing gown.

Houston managed to push the woman back and slice across her arm causing the woman to fall to the floor. As he turned back to Macleod a voice broke through the chaos.

'That's it, boys, in there. The bastard's gone in there. Get him, get him!'

Houston bolted for the door and Macleod slumped to the floor. Only then did it occur to him that the voice that yelled was that of an Ulsterman. Macleod dragged himself to the door and saw Houston in the car trying to make it start. But as much as the ignition sounded, the car would not turn over. Seeing Macleod, the man exited the car and ran back to the trees.

Macleod felt awful, his head still ringing from being driven into the wall but he found his legs. Giving one last glance back to the woman, who was weeping on the floor and apart from a bloody arm seemed okay, he ran after Houston. Macleod was slow, even by his standards, and he suspected Houston would be gone. But then he heard a thump and a yell came from Houston. Then he heard two more thumps.

Macleod staggered through the trees and saw Houston lying on the ground, possibly out cold. His face was a mess, his nose broken and blood ran from it, across his cheeks and hair. Standing several trees back was Smythe with a look of sheer innocence on his face.

'Man ran into a tree, Inspector. Came out here like the

hounds of hell, looked back, probably to see you and then turned right into a tree. Smashed his nose something bad. Wasn't pleasant to see.'

Macleod bent over double and tried to suck in air. When he could, he looked over at Smythe and said, 'A tree? Must have been a blooming big tree.'

'Well, they are. I mean look at them.'

'And he hit it three times from what I heard.'

'Bounced, Seoras. Tragic.'

Macleod grabbed his mobile and dialled the emergency number. As it rang, he shouted to Smythe. 'There's a man in there, sliced neck, see if you can do anything. If not, see to the girl, she'll be pretty shaken.'

He heard the operator ask for which service and he responded. As the call was being connected, Macleod looked at Smythe running down to the house. *Bounced off a tree, as if. Good job, my friend, damn good job.*

Chapter 15

Macleod was feeling frustrated again. It seemed to be happening a lot lately and this time it was the trafficking unit who were in his way. He had generously let them run the operation to bring in Houston and all he had asked for was access to the man quickly after arrest. The manner of his arrest had not helped as the injuries due to *running into a tree three times* had meant that Houston had to receive treatment. Macleod had pressed his case for action as he was on a murder hunt and that more deaths were possible but it was now three in the morning and he was waiting for his information.

The sessions with Houston had been slow and Macleod had watched through the glass as the detectives from the trafficking branch had interviewed the man. It was not that they were incompetent, merely that Macleod was desperate for information to act on. They were now on a recess and with the unit at Cromarty down to a skeleton staff, Macleod had no one to talk to. He had thought about calling Hope but she needed to sleep after her long journey and there was nothing to say. He picked up his mobile and pressed a contact.

'Hello? Who's this?'

'Hi love, it's me, Seoras.'

'Seoras, what's the crisis? Are you okay? What's happened?' Jane's voice was breathless and worried.

'Nothing, I just wanted to chat—see how you were.'

'It's three in the morning, Seoras, are you sure you're okay? Do I need to come to you?'

'No,' said Macleod, a little too quickly, 'I'm just kicking about and realised I hadn't caught up with you. How's the house hunt going?'

'Good, Seoras, good. I saw another four today, no wait, yesterday. I'm seeing three today.' Her voice sounded tired and Macleod thought he had been unwise to wake her. But part of him didn't care; he wanted to hear her encouraging tones about the house move. He was feeling left out of it but at least she was getting around plenty of the properties. She might have to choose too, if the case kept going.

'Any in particular?'

'Yes! I think I found the place. Right by the sea but very secluded. The ground's a bit awkward around it and it's not that big but it's got a great view. And not too far from Inverness. Perfect for your work, if you can get transferred up.'

'Sounds great, love.'

'We can go when you're through with the case. How is it going?'

Macleod said nothing for a moment, wondering if he should simply say *okay* and let that be it. *Heck, she wanted in.* 'I'm just killing time, waiting on information to move. Hope's down south and my other DCs are with Hope or in bed. I'm just killing time.'

'You sound frustrated. How long do you have to wait around?'

'Could be another hour or maybe more until I get the

information.'

'Do you need to be there? I mean, I take it you are at the station.'

'No, I don't really.'

'Shopping centre round from your station. Go there and get me a hot chocolate.'

'Why?' asked Macleod.

'Just do it.'

Having received his orders Macleod did as instructed, letting the trafficking team know where he could be contacted. Twenty minutes later, he was sitting in his car with a coffee and a hot chocolate on his dashboard when he saw a woman round the corner of the car park. She had a rucksack with her and approached his car, opening the boot and throwing the rucksack inside. After removing a large blanket and two pillows, she opened the rear door and sat upright, covering herself with the blanket. Macleod climbed into the rear of the car and positioned himself behind her, holding her tight while she took the drinks.

'You didn't have to do this. Did you bring any of the details about the house?'

'Shut up, it's three-thirty. I'm here for company, not conversation.'

After a ten-minute silence while she drank her chocolate, Jane described the house and how she saw them living there. There were many intimate details about quiet moments they could have as well as ideas about colours and furniture. And then silence, before he heard her light snoring. He knew he would not sleep but this was better than the cafeteria in the station.

At five-thirty his mobile rang and he received a summons to

the station. His back was sore from the angle he'd been sitting at and Jane looked dishevelled as she got up and packed the blanket in the rucksack.

'I'll drop you off,' said Macleod.

'No, it's fine. I need to walk to wake up.'

He held her and kissed her on the forehead, aware that the staff of the shopping centre were now arriving in larger numbers along with a few customers. Feeling self-conscious, he quickly let go of Jane and opened his car door.

'Is that all I get,' she said watching him climb inside the car. 'I come out in the middle of the night and you let me go with a peck to the forehead.'

'There's people about,' said Macleod quickly.

'The hell with them, I deserve more than a hot chocolate for my efforts.' She climbed on top of him and he had no defence as she kissed him hungrily. They were both tired and not in their freshest state but her sheer hunger was intoxicating.

Jane stepped back out of the car and grabbed her rucksack. 'That's how to say goodbye, Macleod, and don't forget it!' Macleod must have looked stunned or embarrassed because she burst out laughing before walking off.

Back at the station, Macleod was invited into the office of DI Masterton of the Trafficking branch. Bacon rolls arrived as Macleod sat down and he hungrily polished one off as Masterton prepared himself.

'Got some good news for you, Macleod. Houston identified your men from photos we gave him. He's up to his neck and he was singing for us. You've brought in a player with this, can't thank you enough. I know you said you had a source; do you think we can talk to the source?'

'I think he'll talk to us if he has anything. But what did

Houston say about my Danish soldiers?' asked Macleod,

'Well, he identified them all but not with the names you have. Borgen, he called Smith, and his main contact with them. He recognised Digman as being with Borgen nearly every time they met. Nyman he had only seen once, but they are connected. They had been using the same supply routes and had exchanged people between them, mainly women for prostitution. But he thinks they operate away from the Inverness area, more to the west side of the country. High end, he said, people with money and big estates.'

'Any places?'

'He met them two days ago in Ullapool. Said they had a van with them which usually meant movement of people.'

'Did he say they were going off the mainland?' asked Macleod.

'He suspected it but could not confirm. It was a dark blue minibus, tinted windows. All three were there. You could check the ferry but I reckon they might have moved them a different way. Harbours would be good to check. Also, airports for movement of the clients.'

Macleod nodded. The net was having to be spread wide now and his resources were looking stretched. 'Masterton, can we run this jointly? I'm going to go to Ullapool but I'm stretched thin, frankly. Can I count on your team to run the telephones and computer searches? My own are already knee deep in crime scenes.'

Masterton stood up and shook Macleod's hand. 'Anything, Macleod, after the fish you just brought us, anything. And don't worry, your guys will get the credit too.'

'Credit's irrelevant,' said Macleod, 'as long as we get them before they kill more.'

Macleod left the office and called Ross to begin to organise his people. Masterton helpfully gave Macleod an officer, DC Duggal, a middle-aged Pakistani woman to assist him. She was dark-skinned and smiled broadly but with a slightly crooked middle tooth. Her long black hair had a silky quality and she was broadly built for a woman.

'Good morning, sir,' said Duggal as she introduced herself to Macleod. 'Do we take your car? I have a bag packed as the boss said we might be a few days if this trail is hot.'

'Morning, Constable. Yes, we'll take my car. I have a change with me. I'm going to have a quick shower before we hit the road. Your boss was going to get the local police to pick up the CCTV from the harbour area and send it here. See how that's going and we'll make tracks.'

The woman nodded and disappeared as Macleod looked for the locker area and stood under a hot shower for ten minutes. His legs were sore and tired but his spirit was up. There was a trail to follow and he was on to it. And if Hope could fill in the details about Fiske they might begin to understand what was actually happening.

The road out of Inverness to Ullapool took Macleod past lochs and forests before reaching a large stretch of moor which seemed to go on forever, the land looking bright in the morning sunshine. There were tourist caravans and motorhomes on the route slowing down their progress but Macleod simply stared at the water of close-by lochs which showed barely a ripple. In this summer climate, he understood why people would flock here.

They descended into Ullapool and found the small town busy with holiday makers. There was a wealth of information walking around and Macleod was glad to see some uniforms questioning the public. Checking in at the local police station, he made sure that CCTV was being acquired and that the local ferry operator was being questioned about the traffic of the previous day. The ferry was just coming around the tip of Ullapool and making its turn to reverse onto the pier.

Macleod was satisfied that things were underway when he was summoned by Duggal to a house a few minutes from the station. It was a detached house with a Bed and Breakfast sign outside that indicated there were no vacancies and a woman was standing looking pensive outside. She was being spoken to by an officer who waved both Duggal and Macleod over.

'This is Mrs Davidson, and she runs Ceol na Mara, a bed and breakfast. It also has a small flat at the end of the house. She says it has been occupied for the last two days by two women, one middle aged and one barely beyond her teens. They seem to match the description of the women you have been looking for, sir.

'Yesterday, about four o'clock, the girl left the house. The couple were meant to leave this morning and they should have been out by nine as Mrs Davidson has another client coming. When they did not drop the keys off, she tried to make contact with them by banging on the door. When this did not work she looked in through the window and saw one of the women, apparently dead.

'And did you break in?' asked Macleod.

'Yes, sir.'

'And?'

'Come and see for yourself.'

The officer led Macleod to a white door and then gently pushed it ajar. He stepped aside, inviting Macleod in. On a bed was a woman he thought looked like an older version of

Anna Fiske. Her neck was twisted at an angle that said it was broken and she was pale. The smell of death was in the air and Macleod reared at it. There was nothing else there except the body.

Why kill her? Who was this other woman?

Chapter 16

Hope stretched her back and looked out at the coastline. The south of England was so very different to the highlands, different even to Glasgow. It was now the afternoon and they had started the day with an interview with Maltman, the man whose name had come up in Amundsen's photographs. Meeting him was quite an experience and one that Hope wished to forgo next time. He was slime, talking about the girls in the photos, relishing every comment, leering at the pictures. He 'sampled the merchandise' as he put it and she was one of his favourites. However, he had been sad to trade her further north.

A name, Houston, had been mentioned as one of the men he had passed her on to, and Macleod confirmed he had the man in custody but not the girl from the photograph. Macleod explained he was in pursuit of Freja Fiske but the location of the three Danish soldiers was still unknown. With that trail running hot up north, Hope decided to continue to Kent to find out more about the adopted child, Liva Amundsen. The address of the new parents on the adoption paper was in Kent. The adoption was nearly twenty years ago and Hope was not sure if the couple on the papers would still be at this address.

The house on the edge of Dover had a quaint garden around

it that was in full bloom. With the colours generated by the flowers, one could have missed the tired facia and rotting window edges that told of somewhere dilapidated rather than a country paradise. Allinson joined Hope in walking up the gravel drive and they knocked on the door. When no answer was forthcoming, Hope pressed the doorbell but she could not hear it ring. Then a crunch of small stones made them turn and they saw an elderly man, possibly in his seventies.

'Yes, can I help you?' The voice was croaky, and a little hoarse. The man was puffing hard as if coming around the side of his house had been an effort. Despite the sun shining and the temperature making even Hope sweat, the man was sporting a thick cardigan and brown trousers. In his hand was a small trowel.

'Detectives McGrath and Allinson, sir. I was wondering if we could ask you a few questions?'

'You're not from here, are you, dear? That sounds like a Scottish accent. Are you from Scotland?' The man did not seem very cogent and Hope wondered just how much use he was going to be.

'We are looking into the details of a person and we think you may have adopted her as a child, about twenty years ago.'

'No, not me. It was my wife and I who adopted a child. Pretty little girl. She was sweet but was too hard for us to handle. We were already getting old.' The man waved his hand for them to follow and then trudged off around the side of the house. The pair followed and they arrived in the back garden and saw a cast iron table that was suffering from flaking white paint. Collapsing into a chair, the man waved at them to sit and took a moment to catch his breath.

'Now, I'm Reggie, and my wife's Dolly. The Myercrofts, that's us, been here for over fifty years now. Bought the house with my own money back in the day when Dolly said she wanted to marry. Done us proud, the old girl. Takes a bit now to keep on top of but then the wife loves the house.'

'Is your wife at home?' asked Hope.

'She's here.' The man looked around him as if searching everything.

'Could we speak to her, too?'

'Hardly, love. Dolly died some time ago. That's when I had to give up the young girl you mentioned.'

'But you said your wife was here,' blurted Allinson before Hope could stop him.

'Yes, son. You see she's in this house, in the flowers, she's with me right here. Dolly picked that flower bed over there. Not my colours at all but she wanted it that way. And this table, picked by her hand. We had many a time out here in the sun. When you get older, you find out that people are never gone, they're just speaking to you in a different way.'

Although finding the man's sentiment was clutching at her emotions, Hope needed information and so decided to try and pin the man down instead of letting him meander along with his thoughts.

'Did you ever meet the parents of the child you adopted?' asked Hope.

'Several times. They were a foreign couple, Scandinavian, but they were okay despite that. The man had a military background. The mother found it hard but never resented us. She would just tell us all about the girl and what she ate, and how to get her to sleep. I think there were four or maybe five visits before we took over.'

Hope took out some photographs from her pocket, of Malthe

126

and Anna Fiske from their army days. She placed them before the man and saw the instant recognition in his eyes.

'That was her, love. A good-looking girl, she was. Dolly liked her too. He was very matter of fact but you could tell she was a real mother, not one of these fly-by-night girls, not someone who has had a bit of a fling and wants to simply move on. That was important to us. You had to be sure of what sort of stock you were getting, didn't you?'

The old man laughed and then dropped into a burst of coughing which made Hope wonder about his overall health. When he had recovered, Hope took the photographs away and placed the photograph of the naked girl that Amundsen had fixated on but she covered up the body with her hand.

'Do you recognise this woman?'

'I haven't seen her face before but she looks very like the mother who brought us Liva. Amundsens, they were; did I say that already? She's older and it looks like she has had some life experience but that could be Liva. She was young when she left us.'

The man suddenly snatched the photograph and brought it to his face. His eyes began to water and he suddenly burst into tears. 'Is that what she's become? Showing herself to all and sundry,' he wailed. 'She was such a beautiful child. If Dolly was here, we'd have seen her right, she would not be like this. Why did you have to bring me this? That was something good in our life and now you tell me it was for nothing, that she's gone off the rails.'

'Could I ask—' began Allinson.

'No, you cannot, sir. Just get out. I have little enough here without you wrecking what little I have to hold on to. Get out, the pair of you.' And the man was on his feet and shooing them both. Hope nodded to Allinson and they beat a hasty retreat. As they crunched their way down the drive they could still hear the old man crying.

'That could have gone better,' said Hope.

'But we know that the girl in the photo is Anna's child,' said Allinson, 'and that she's ended up in the hands of the three soldiers again. You can understand why Anna Fiske was after them. Imagine your child, born from them now being abused by them, after you were also their play thing.'

'I'll call it in to Macleod, and we had better start heading north again.'

Allinson drove the car back out of the busy city of Dover, amazed at the amount of traffic on the roads. 'I couldn't live here,' he said.

'Glasgow can be this busy,' said Hope. 'You should see the main motorway as it snakes through the centre. At rush hour it's a fight to cruise across and get the right exit.'

'It would have to be a hell of a woman to get me to live here.'

There was silence in the car as the elephant in the back seat roared loudly. Allinson stared hard at the road ahead while Hope took out her mobile. 'I'll call the boss then,' she said.

The silence continued as Hope waited for an answer to her call. Macleod was usually prompt but this time, he was an age and she was panicking that she may have to address the unanswered question in the car.

'Hope, it's Macleod. Sorry, I'm just getting onto the ferry so had to run up the stairs before I answered. How did you get on?'

'It turns out that Amundsen and Fiske went together to put up Anna Fiske's child for adoption, I think they may even have registered the child as Amundsen's. She seemed to have quite a hold over him. The child, Liva, was adopted by a couple, the Myercrofts, and after six years the adopted mother died so the child was moved on. Struggling for records after that, so not sure how she went into foster care but if she was using Amundsen we might find her more easily now. Anyway, seems she's gotten back into the hands of the soldiers and that seems like a good reason for revenge of some sort.'

'Agreed, and for the soldiers to try and cover it up by killing Amundsen. It seems Malthe got caught in the middle and paid the price. I'm on the ferry because we caught footage of Freja Fiske going onto the boat. She's on Lewis, we believe they may be on Lewis. I've alerted the station over there but the ferry had already unloaded, so she's loose over there. And we don't know where our soldiers are.'

'Are they working or hiding?' asked Hope.

'I think they are working. So, I'll be checking anywhere that can hold a small crowd but there's a lot of ground and not a lot of resources here. I've got Stornoway checking CCTV footage, bus footage and that. She didn't have a car but we know she's perfectly capable of stealing one. It looks like she dispatched her mother when she was in pain, so Freja has no qualms about killing.'

'I'm on my way back up but it'll take a while. Do you want me to join you?'

'Yes, both of you. Allinson worked here for a few years so he'll be very handy and I'll keep Ross back on the mainland.'

Hope heard the tension in Macleod's voice. 'What's up, Seoras? Are you okay?'

'No, I'm not. I don't see a good outcome on this one. We usually save this one or that person who didn't deserve this or that. Here, apart from the girl who's been trafficked, there's no good outcome. And even for her, her half-sister's about to kill her dad.'

'Let's just stop the bloodbath,' said Hope, 'that's all you can do. We'll drive through the night and fly over in the morning. Let me know if anything further develops.'

Hope switched off the call and looked over at Allinson who was still watching the road. He was tense, clearly worried that what had been said was going to drive a wedge, that he had put his foot right into it.

'I wouldn't want to live here either,' said Hope, throwing out a line to the man.

'You more a Glasgow girl,' said Allinson.

'I don't know,' said Hope. 'I've been there for so long but working out of the city has given me a liking for these mountains and coastlines, up north. I've been wondering about moving up to somewhere a little less busy.'

'There's nowhere like it to live. I enjoyed the island but I still needed the city close by. 'Allinson was now in full flow and Hope eased as he regaled all about highland life. When he had finished, Hope curled up in her seat and looked back at him.

'You know, I could do with someone to show me around the place, help me find somewhere to stay if I moved. Could do with a friend up there.'

Allinson smiled. 'If you need a friend, I'm in. You can count on me to give you a hand and show you around.'

'Good,' said Hope, 'friends it is. For starters anyway.' *He's just too easy to be around.*

Chapter 17

The ferry across the Minch had been surprisingly rough for the time of year and Macleod had remained in his seat for much of the trip. His colleague, DC Duggal, seemed to be a natural sailor and had happily wandered around the vessel, bringing Macleod back coffee and a snack on demand. But as they sailed into Stornoway harbour, Macleod raised himself and stood out on deck with the younger officer.

'Ever been on Lewis, Duggal?'

'No, sir. There hasn't been much call to visit on account of work and my family is spread out across several of the UK's cities. My parents and their brothers and sisters have worked in retail, mainly selling, but these days that has changed.'

Duggal's hair was tied tight in a knot at the rear of her head but it still had that shininess to it that Macleod marvelled at. He wondered if it came from a bottle or if it was a natural effect. His hair had long since lost any lustre and he thought himself jealous. Growing up on Lewis, he had encountered few Asian people but since he transferred to Glasgow, he had become more aware of their culture and thought himself so ignorant before when he would have had naive thoughts about people of a different skin.

The boat sailed past Holm and Macleod looked over at the

life ring on the white mounting, standing alone with only a single beach angler some distance away. This was where Hope and he had ended their first case and the shock of the cold water when he had jumped in was a feeling that didn't dim. But then this was also where he had lost his wife. Macleod stood with his head bowed for a moment whispering a prayer to his God.

'Some said you were a religious man, sir.'

Macleod opened his eyes. 'Some?'

'At the station. They had been at Glasgow, knew you from there. Said you were strongly conservative in your beliefs.'

'Not as much these days, Duggal, a little less confident, and maybe a bit more secure.' Macleod was aware that he was being very cryptic but he was not up for a debate on religion. His whole view of his faith had been shaken in these last years and he was not ready to bare his soul to the world. It was hard enough to let Jane see his worries and failure to understand his God. And she was a fellow believer.

'Faith is hard, sir. I bet they mocked you for it. They do that to me. At least I'm different all over—can't be easy for someone from here.'

Macleod looked at the officer, trying to gauge if she was winding him up but there was no malice in her eyes; instead she seemed to be sad about the fact. 'It is, Duggal. Thank you.' The Coastguard station passed before them and then the new marina before the ferry sailed onto its berth. They made their way downstairs to the car. Macleod drove to the station and the pair joined a middle-aged DC for a briefing.

'Name's Harper, sir. I have everything moving for you. We are reviewing CCTV from town as she must have walked off the ferry. There's two working on that in the room up the corridor. As for your other miscreants, I have officers asking around the various harbours and jetties we have, but if you're from here, sir, you'll know that we are chasing a needle in a haystack. I doubt their boat would have displayed any AIS, so tracing them would be hard.'

'AIS?' asked Duggal.

'Automatic Identification System,' said Harper. 'Vessels over a certain size have to display it but it's available to all vessels to have. Handy for seeing who is around you, avoiding collisions and that but not good if you want to remain covert. I have the Coastguard checking recent traffic across the Minch but it's unlikely to yield much. We don't even know what vessel we are looking for.'

'Unlikely but keep searching,' insisted Macleod. 'Get the Ullapool harbourmaster to give you the last week's record of movements, see who came in and then went out around the time of our traffickers being there. Then get Stornoway's records see if there's a match. Check the other harbours and jetties for a match too. It's a long shot but if it comes off we could get very lucky indeed.'

Harper nodded as a plain clothes officer arrived and excused herself to Macleod and asked to see Harper. Instead of leaving, Harper introduced DC Smith and then asked the young woman to tell her message.

'We have a hit on the CCTV, or at least what looks like her. Just after two o'clock entering the sports centre. She goes in and then comes out at four. Her hair is wet and tied up and she has an extra bag. We're trying to trace that bag on the CCTV, see who brought it in. Checking the cameras outside in the car park now to try and get further about our suspect too.'

'Good,' said Macleod. 'Duggal, with me. We'll go the Sports

centre, Harper, and see what we can find. Get through the rest of the CCTV in the area, see if she gets into a car or jumps on the bus, or whatever. Keep me informed.'

Soon they were approaching the sports centre doors and Macleod asked at reception for the manager. He wanted to keep things low key and thought speaking to a man he had seen before would help.

The sports centre manager, Mr Maclean, was dressed in a shirt and tie and shook Macleod's hand with apprehension. 'Hello, Inspector, it's good to see you again but I worry why. Your officers picked up our CCTV files earlier.'

'We have a suspect who came into the centre about two o'clock and then left around four. Is the same shift still on as I would like to question them? I don't want to disturb you unduly so I'll just have a quiet word with your lifeguards one by one and then ask for them to be withdrawn if I need them further.'

'Okay,' said Maclean, 'as you wish but I'll get an extra one at poolside as they have a job to do and I imagine you'll be quite distracting.'

Maclean led them through to the changing area before the swimming pool. At the end of the area, he insisted they put on shoe covers before going poolside and then introduced them to the first lifeguard before he wandered off to explain to the others.

'Hi, I'm DI Macleod; this is DC Duggal,' said Macleod to the white-haired woman who sat on an upright chair before him, beside the arm bands and floats. He fumbled inside his jacket and pulled an artist's drawing of Freja Fiske out, unfolding it before the woman. 'I'd like you to take a look at this picture and tell me if you saw this woman today.'

The woman stared and then looked off, trying to think. 'Yes, I did. She was here, I remember her in the shower just as I went off break and then I remember her leaving the health suite later. I can't remember the time exactly but she came out of the suite with another woman.'

'What did the other woman look like?' asked Duggal.

'She was thin and pale, freckly skin. She had light red hair too. I've seen her about before but not the other girl. I don't remember them being together when I first saw the girl in the picture but they seemed to be laughing and joking when they left. They washed off in the shower over there before disappearing to the lockers. That's the last I saw of them. Matt would have been on when I left for my break that first time. Ask him if they were together?'

'Matt?' asked Macleod.

'Far end on the really high stool. He might even know the pale girl—he's the right age.'

Macleod and Duggal walked along the poolside to the far end where they found Matt looking down at them from on high. He nodded at them and then stared back at the pool.

'Can I ask you to come down, sir, I need to talk to you?'

The man nodded. He was in his early twenties, Macleod guessed, if not younger but he had a strapping physique and a mop of curly brown hair. He descended the steps of the high chair quickly and stood beside the pair of detectives.

'Hello sir, I need you to look at this picture and tell me if you recognise this girl,' said Macleod.

'Of course, you're the detectives that Mr Maclean was talking about. No problem.' The man looked down at the image and then nodded profusely. 'Oh yes, I remember her. She came in as I came back from break. Kind of caught the eye.'

Macleod wondered if she really did catch the eye or was the man at that stage in life where every woman catches his eye. But at least his hormones may lead to a bit of information.

'And what did she do?'

'Well, she stood in the shower for a bit, quite a while actually, looking out across the pool. It wasn't that busy but we had a few people in, mainly oldies and that. Aqua aerobics was starting.'

'And after that?' asked Duggel.

'She got into the pool and started swimming up and down. Was on her own. The aerobics classes started so the top of the pool was being used with that. A school was in using a side section of the pool and so we got busy. But there was only her and two men in the other part of the pool. Then Catherine came in.'

'Catherine? Who's that?' asked Duggel

'Three years below me in school and now just started working at the supermarket. Not the cleverest girl but nice. Very sweet and good for a laugh. She's just got herself mobile and I think has a flat out of town now, somewhere. I mean, I know her to look at and say hello to, but I don't know much about her since I left school. You know how it is when you're not around people.'

'And what happened with Catherine?' asked Macleod.

'Well, they got to talking, I remember that, but then I got involved with a disabled woman needing help. Next thing I was doing my rounds and walked past the window that looks into the Jacuzzi. The two of them were sitting in it, chatting away, really intently. I remember they got out about half three and showered for a bit before going to get changed. I think they used the same cubicle. We have doubles for families so they shouldn't really use it but I reckon they went in together. Sorry, you just notice these things.'

Duggal asked something else but Macleod's blood ran cold. He pulled out his mobile phone and dialled the station. 'Get me Harper!'

'Excuse me, sir,' said Matt, 'you can't use that mobile in here.'

'Shut up, kid,' said Macleod and then heard Duggel, explaining something to the lifeguard.

'Harper.'

'Harper, get in the CCTV room and check Fiske when she exits. Is there anything different about her and is she with someone? Also check for a red head, very pale and thin, young girl of about eighteen or so leaving around then.'

'Yes, sir.'

'And Harper, quickly, it's important. I'll hold the line.'

Macleod was standing for ten minutes, his heart pounding. 'Matt, show Duggal the changing room they used.' As Macleod continued to wait he watched the pair walk off. *Please be wrong,* he thought, *dear God, let me wrong.*

'Sir, Harper. We checked the CCTV and no one leaves with her. The only difference I can see is she has a different bag. It's the same colour, blue, but it's a different size, smaller.'

'And the red head?'

'Clocked a pale girl coming in about two thirty, but she doesn't leave, cannot find her leaving before five o'clock.'

'Thank you, Harper.'

'Sir . . .'

But Macleod had switched off the mobile and was waving at Mr Maclean who was watching the pool. 'The locker keys, Maclean, get me the locker keys.'

'Sure, but why?'

'Just do it!' roared Macleod. *Let me be wrong, let me be wrong, God, please!*

Maclean hurried back with the keys and Macleod steered him towards Duggal and Matt who were standing outside a changing cubicle before some lockers. They all had keys in them except for one.

'That one, Maclean. Open it and then stand back, please.'

Maclean obliged and Macleod held the thin door ajar, while he looked inside. He saw a blue bag. Reaching inside he pulled at it but it was heavy.

'Duggal, a hand.'

Together they pulled the bag out from the locker, although it caught several times on the way out. Tumbling onto the floor, you could see the odd shapes poking at the bag giving it an unnatural shape for a receptacle that contained swimming apparel or clothing of any type.

'Stand back,' shouted Macleod to the manager and the lifeguard. 'Right back, now.'

Macleod pulled back the zipper on the bag and saw a pale arm and then a shock of red hair.

'No!'

Chapter 18

Macleod stood at the harbour side in Stornoway town and looked at the white and black ferry that had brought him over the previous day. Already the cars were assembling for this trip back across the Minch to Ullapool and the town was coming alive. There was a distinct degree of shock occurring too. Anyone who had used the lockers for the swimming pool would know what they looked like and could visualise someone stuffed inside, albeit in a bag.

Catherine turned out to be a quiet woman who had been struggling socially and maybe that was what Freja Fiske had preyed upon. But why kill her for a car? Why not simply steal one? It would have been easier and it would have brought less attention. It seemed to Macleod that this girl enjoyed killing. If she had been simply after these Danish soldiers, as horrible as any murder is, at least they might have deserved their deaths. But this was an innocent, and he had been too slow to stop it.

He was standing beside the sea wall with his back to a pub that his friends had frequented in youth but which still had the same white facade. Days like these he saw the value of drink, that ability to simply drown himself so the pain became numb. But it was temporary and the pain would always be there in the morning. His elation of helping the trafficked women from the two days previous had dwindled to become a self-deprecating should-have-done-better.

His eyes caught sight of the wooden posts in the sea beside the wall. They were shaped like a simple boat, apparently the size of a vessel that had gone down on New Year at the end of World War One, islanders returning home from the war. They never made it. The ship foundered on the Beasts of Holm, not far from where his own wife died. *Loss was always with us, but God, why the hell this girl?*

Duggal had suggested the walk to Macleod after he was getting into the faces of the nightshift at Stornoway police station. And she was right. He was raging at the girl's death, frustrated at not finding Fiske or the car, despite pulling on resources from the other emergency services. Exhausted, Macleod was at the end of his tether and needed to release some anger. And so, he looked around for a suitable moment before yelling briefly at the sea. Then he calmly turned and walked back to the station.

Hope and Allinson were due in on the first plane, having driven up the previous day from the south of England and arriving at Inverness in the small hours of the morning. It would be good to have Hope here. Duggal was a good officer but conversation was stilted and she did not contest his theories without giving him too much respect. When it came to solving the case, Macleod thought he needed no respect and everyone should simply throw in their thoughts. Whether he actually promoted this deliberately or unconsciously was another matter. But with Hope, that was what he got.

The other side of the case was proving as difficult as the first, with no progress made on the vessel that would have carried the soldiers over with their potential cargo of trafficked women. For this, he had asked the Coastguard to assist and they were duly checking up on vessel movements where they could, sending teams round harbours to note vessels that were there. Local fishermen were also questioned as they were a great source of knowing the regular marine traffic from the abnormal. But this side had been overshadowed by the death of the young local woman and he needed to make sure it was thoroughly chased up; after all, they may find their killer by finding her prey first.

It was nine o'clock when Hope walked into the temporary operations room in the station and she looked exhausted too. Her hair was tied up in a ponytail but it was roughly done. She wore jeans and a grey jumper that sat neatly under her leather jacket. Without engaging anyone else she made a beeline for Macleod's desk.

'Anything new?'

Macleod shook his head. 'We have everyone out looking, pulling CCTV from everywhere. I reckon she's gone to ground.'

'No,' said Hope, 'why would she go to ground? She's on a hunt; she doesn't care about being hunted.'

'Why not? If she's caught, it's over. She cares too much for that.'

'From what you have told me about her actions when being pursued,' said Hope, 'I think she's throwing you off her trail.'

'How do you mean?'

'Well, she cleans up all the loose ends rather coldly. The girl at Embo. I think this murder was to get us running around chasing her here when she calmly goes elsewhere.'

'She'd kill just for that.'

'She dispatched her mother when she was about to become

141

a liability, whether that was agreed or not. The other thing is that we have assumed she is on the trail of these soldiers. That, I agree with. With her mother, she killed Malthe, possibly for his actions in earlier times. She was tailing him, hence the opportunistic killing on the ferry. But she doesn't know what Borgen, Digman, and Nyman look like. They were all on the ferry in the small cabin as they crossed. She could have gone wild and done the lot there and then.'

'But she doesn't know what they look like,' said Macleod. 'Her mother would have only had memories from twenty years ago. Malthe knew them but he's stuck on a ferry because they got on last. Maybe he thinks he can handle it or that in public the women won't do anything. Maybe he's resigned to his fate or he thinks he can escape by car.'

'And when she attacks him on the ferry, Malthe is already poisoned, so he can't react to her attack.'

'So, if she doesn't know them, why is she here? She must be on their trail too, in some respect. There is somewhere here that they use. If we trail them, she'll come to us.'

'Which is great if she doesn't dispatch more red herrings in the meantime,' said Macleod. 'So, we need to keep on the random search for Freja Fiske, in case we find her by luck. But our efforts need to be focused on the soldiers, what they look like and where they would go. They knew Malthe was on to them. I reckon that was why he hired Smythe.'

'What do you mean?' asked Hope.

'Malthe must have investigated, looking for the daughter. Anna Fiske must have made contact. Then Malthe goes looking and he is identified by the soldiers as looking into their business. So he gets an operator like Smythe who can work without being detected. But it's too late—they are coming after him.'

'But the question remains, where on these islands would you set up a forced brothel? You have to keep the women out of sight, but you need to be within reach. If it was a cheap job and you were packing people through the doors then you would be on the mainland.'

'It won't be in town,' said Macleod. 'It'll be out in the remote parts. It could be the Westside, out on the coast. Or maybe Berneray, Aird Uig, Reef. Or maybe Harris, the east side of it. There's plenty here.'

'Or it might be the islands further down. All we know is they were going out of Ullapool.'

'No, it's Lewis or Harris. They would have gone from Skye otherwise.' Macleod thought for a moment then shouted across the room. 'Duggal, come here a moment, please.' The dark-skinned woman hurried over. 'Duggal, if you were running a brothel here, or whatever sort of operation they have for these women, what sort of clients would you have?'

'Well it's pretty remote, so you need someone willing to pay, able to get here. Although I thought those sorts of people might be a little too ostentatious for here. They would show up on the radar.'

'You'd certainly get noticed flying here in your jet, or arriving on your large yacht or boat,' said Macleod. 'The locals would spot you a mile off.'

'But maybe if you ran something different,' said Duggal. 'Make it a tourist trip, make it somewhere that looks like any other tourist venture and keep it all behind closed doors. So, we need somewhere large but secreted. I'll get some of the team and get on it. I'll also see if the wider network has anything.'

As Duggal went back to her desk, Macleod leaned back in

his chair. 'What are you thinking?' asked Hope.

'Patrick Smythe. He's been investigating this for Malthe, or at least was. Maybe he might have something, or maybe he could find out. I mean, if you were to run something like this, there are networks and that to promote it.'

Macleod picked up his mobile and found a number Smythe had given him in case he needed any statements or further assistance with the case. The number rang four times and then cut off. As Macleod went to redial a different number came up on his mobile, one he didn't know.

'Hello Inspector, how can I help you?'

Macleod could hear the sea in the background, waves crashing against the shore. 'I take it the scenery's good,' said Macleod. 'I could do with a little help.'

Macleod explained the situation and there was silence on the other end of the phone. Macleod wondered if the line had gone dead but he still heard the constant crash of the waves. 'Are you there?'

'Shush, I'm thinking.'

There was another long pause and a seagull could be heard calling in the distance. Smythe coughed a few times and then Macleod heard him walking along something that sounded wooden. Then he was inside, the waves now more distant, almost muted. As Macleod held the line, he heard water falling into something and then a click.

'Are you making a coffee?'

'Shush!'

Macleod put the mobile on speaker mode and started to absent-mindedly look at some of the paperwork on his desk. The man was taking the mickey, surely. There was water being poured and then a slurp as Smythe drank something.

'Shilton, a lawyer from Birmingham I think. He was with Hughes, Kyle, and Brotherton lawyers. He had signed up from something in the Hebrides. Find him and you might find it.'

'What's he like?'

'How the hell should I know, never met him. It was at a meet they were having and I overheard it being said. Not something I noted down but it was there. Sorry, I had to dig that one up. I remembered the Hebrides bit but extracting the rest from this brain takes time. I'm sure your Traffic guys can get on to him and find something. But that's it. I never found anything connected to the Hebrides otherwise.'

'Great, Smythe, that's a needle worth pursuing anyway. Where are you anyway?'

'Anywhere I'm needed, Inspector. Have to go.'

And with that the line cut off. Macleod called Duggal over and asked her to route the information through her boss to the Birmingham force and see what they could find from the man. He then sat back in his chair somewhat happier and less frustrated than he had been before. But he knew the days would get harder before they got better.

As if on cue, Harper flew into the room clutching a piece of paper, calling for Macleod. 'Sir, sir, we found it; we have the car that she stole. It's in Berneray, small house on its own. Neighbours saw some activity this morning and called their friend to see if everything was all right. They say he had stayed the night in town when they spoke. Uniform went over and found the car but no one else there.'

'Get the photofit out to officers and stop all buses in that area or routing out from there. Get someone down to Tarbet in case she's gone that way, and someone at the bus station in Stornoway. If Freja Fiske is moving, it will be a good chance to catch her.' Macleod rose from his desk and turned to Hope. 'Come on!'

'Where?'

'What do you mean, where?' raged Macleod.

'And what do you mean, come on! Where are we going, sir?'

'To the car, then to wherever they find her.'

'No, uniform have the car; they can search the house but I doubt she even used anything. We need to get on a map and start looking at a search. But a general one, she's too dangerous to have people be close to her.'

Hope was right and Macleod knew it. They needed to cast a net and see if she was caught. He just wanted to get moving; he was always two steps behind on this case and people died when he could not get in front.

'Get a map, get a desk, and start plotting,' he said to Hope. 'Allinson, give her a hand and show me what you have in twenty minutes time.' As the pair turned away, he grabbed Hope's arm and whispered in her ear, 'Sorry.'

She nodded and then followed Allinson. Macleod returned to his seat for twenty minutes studying reports and then joined Hope and Allinson at their desk. They had plotted possible routes by road and over ground that she could have followed. If only he knew roughly where she was going then they would have a better chance of intercepting her.

The car was seen on Berneray; the small island was saturated but nothing else came up. By lunchtime, Macleod was more frustrated than before and had taken another walk to try and focus himself once again. Hope and Allinson were doing a great job of marshalling the troops and making sure every part of the process was in check. As he walked and once more stood at the sea wall looking out, his mobile rang.

'Yes, Duggal.'

'Sir, have had word from the team in Birmingham. They managed to find Mr Shilton and he folded almost immediately. It was a rumour he heard when online on the dark web and he met a man who he gave several thousand pounds to. He's meant to be coming up to the island in two-months' time, but he doesn't know where. There're no photographs of any place, just of some of the girls. They are pretty graphic and it's all very sordid, even for trafficking.'

'Can we use him to get to them?'

'No, they are to contact him,' said Duggal. 'We are tracing through websites and that, but it's not easy going and if they are taking large amounts of money, they are usually very sophisticated.'

'Did he say anything about the place or that?'

'No, he doesn't know where he's even going; they were to arrange all travel. He's never been to the Hebrides in his life.'

'Send the photos up and we'll get some of the local team to have a look, see if we can see anything.'

When Macleod returned to the station, photographs were on a table in a separate room. He had seen many things in his time but these were sick in the extreme. He had no idea how sections of the force worked with this sort of thing day in, day out.

'Utter bastards,' said Hope. 'What sort of pleasure do you get in that?'

'I don't know, Hope. I really don't.' Macleod felt himself becoming despondent. They were on the trail but it was rapidly becoming cold. They couldn't search every house on both islands.

'Sir,' said Allinson, 'got a report from Tarbet. I think she's in

Harris.'

'Explain, please?' asked Macleod.

'The officer we stationed at Tarbet interviewed a driver who was on his second run of the day. But on the first run, which he said we had stopped and searched, there had been two girls, or rather young women. They had been chatting and it had sounded like they didn't know each other but were getting close. Both were backpackers.'

'Did one of them match the photofit?'

'Not at first. She had the wrong colour of hair but then the driver coloured the hair in, imagined it tied up and put a pair of glasses on her, thick rimmed. He said he thought it was her, not totally confident but a strong possibility.'

'Okay, get descriptions of both circulated and we're on our way. Hope, with me; Allinson, hold the fort here with Harper. If she's backpacking I want a helicopter too. We need to find this pair and fast, everyone. If we don't, we'll have a second innocent victim on the island.'

Chapter 19

The drive to Tarbet on the Isle of Harris was only forty minutes but it passed through the moorland of the isle of Lewis before reaching the hills of Harris. Although not completely flat, the land had that endless feel, like it would stretch forever, despite Lewis being relatively small. The change on arrival in Harris was stark, with the Clisham, the tallest of the Harris hills, looking resplendent in sunlight. This was a treat which did not go unnoticed by Macleod as the standard weather in the area meant that it was usually surrounded in drizzle and topped with cloud.

'How are you doing, Hope?' asked Macleod to his partner behind the wheel. It was just the two of them for the first time since Hope arrived. Macleod thought she looked tired, her hair not as neat as usual. Not that Hope ever looked bad, even in a poor light. But she seemed to be straining to keep going. He knew the feeling, his legs playing up due to the lack of sleep.

'Good, I'm fine. Bit knackered after the drive up from England. Allinson and I split it but I struggle to sleep in a car seat. What about you? Bit of a pisser on Jane, you getting pulled away from your holiday.'

'She's busy, house hunting.' He watched Hope's grin and kept a stolid face.

'You kept that quiet. You thinking of moving up north?'

Macleod shook his head. 'Not thinking. I'm doing it. Going to take the plunge with Jane. She's daft enough to want me to, so I can't really refuse.' Again Hope watched his sombre face but he could not hold the expression and broke into a smile.

'That's great, Seoras, really great. She's a really sweet woman.'

'Will you miss me?' asked Macleod.

Hope grinned and Macleod thought she was about to mock him. But she was rarely that cruel. 'I might be going north myself. I need to get away from Glasgow after these last three months.'

Macleod narrowed his eyes in concern. 'Are you really okay?'

'I will be. I thought going north was a good idea; after all, I've seen a lot of the place in the last year. And I've got friends up north.'

'Really?' said Macleod. 'I thought everyone you knew was basically Glasgow. I'm sure you told me that.'

'Maybe I did. But I need to get away and change up my friends, I think. I wanted to settle down in Glasgow and it didn't work out. He just used me and dumped me, Seoras. I need a bit of space to get away and a bit of companionship.'

'Well, you're always welcome at our place when we get it. I know we're older and you and I work together but I still think we can help you . . .'

'Seoras,' interrupted Hope, 'I meant a male companion, someone close, not a friend. I'm glad you see us as friends, and I do too, but there's someone who's been good to me and he deserves a shot at making it something more. I do too.'

'Good,' said Macleod briskly. He was delighted for Hope but

he did not want too much detail. He was a man who enjoyed the frolics of married, or now unmarried life, but some things should be private. 'I'm happy for you, and I'm happy for me. You're a good officer, more than good—I was not happy to be leaving you in Glasgow.'

Hope remained quiet and Macleod watched the car descend the steep road towards Tarbet. On his right, he saw the fishing farm in the sea loch and the road towards Hushinish. It struck him that this place where the men were taking the trafficked women could be anywhere on Harris. And while it was not the largest island that ever existed, it had plenty of small coves and remote houses. Would the outside look any different to a normal dwelling? He doubted it, based on the house that they raided on the Black Isle.

The community hall in Tarbet had become the centre of their searches and was set back off the main square of the town. Tarbet was a lot smaller than Stornoway but it still had a small harbour of its own from which a ferry ran to Skye. It had recently opened new pontoons and had a current influx of yachts and motor boats. The amount of people floating around the town defied its size and Macleod understood what the holiday season meant to a place such as this.

It was late evening and the sun was setting when Macleod had a meal at the local hotel. One thing about long investigations such as this was that you had to keep yourself fit and healthy or you missed things. Sacrificing a meal could leave you drained at that critical juncture. He had sent Hope before him and now left her in charge of the operation as he ate his chicken with chips. Never one for glamourous food, Macleod tried to ignore the excited babble of holiday makers, questioning why there were police officers around asking questions and showing sketches to people.

As he sat finishing his diet cola, Macleod saw an officer come in and approach the barman. The conversation seemed polite and routine until Macleod saw the barman's face change. The officer was taking out his notebook as the man nodded and pointed a finger at the drawing. Jumping out of his seat, Macleod walked briskly to the bar, introduced himself to the barman, and asked the officer to continue.

'Gentleman has said that our party was in here only an hour ago with three other women,' said the police officer. 'Go on, please, sir.'

'I think she was with another back packer, that's what it looked like, although all four came in together. I remember that I thought they were not all one party as two had rucksacks and looked like they had been travelling and the other two were dressed in shorts and tops with trainers or deck shoes, the sailing ones. But they were getting on great. They ordered full meals and then left.'

'What did they look like?' asked the officer. 'Their face, their hair, anything distinctive.'

'To be honest, the two sailing types stuck in my mind. Both brunettes and they looked like twins although I couldn't be sure. Brunettes, small pert noses, quite petite, really. Looked really cute. And English accents, south of England, not that Yorkshire accent or any of that. This was very fine, very properly spoken. Not toffs but that accent with less of the posh words.'

'And the other two?' asked the officer.

'Not so sure what they looked like. Blonde, a dirty blonde one of them. She was European, I think. As for the other one I'm struggling. I remember she had thick-rimmed glasses but otherwise I can't say for sure. But all of them early twenties at best.'

'Officer, stay here and ask the rest of the guests in case anyone has been here for a while. I'm going back to base and I'll pass this on. I think we need to search the local yachts.'

Macleod strode quickly back to the small hub and explained the situation to Hope. Then he called the main base in Stornoway asking for any help they could get to search for these women. Fiske had killed already to cover her tracks and he did not want another murder on his hands.

A group of officers was sent to the pontoons and requested to search for the women but after an hour they returned with negative results. There were a few boats that had not responded and whose owners were possibly walking ashore and an officer had been based there to catch these people when returning. It was now dark and further assistance arrived in the form of the Coastguard. Macleod dispatched them with police officers in small groups to search further out from the pontoons, for any vessels not berthed in the harbour, or who may be at other anchorages.

He was back to a waiting game. Macleod had deployed his pieces and now was awaiting results. He hated this part—hated waiting and would rather be out there searching. He paced the small hall, watching parties return, one after another with no positive result.

During this time, he received a call from Allinson, giving good news about the Danish soldiers and what had happened to the trafficked women they were with. A fisherman had spotted a vessel loading some women and men at Lochinver. The vessel was a motor boat, large by anyone's standards and it had been seen close to Rodel, the previous evening. At least they were searching in the right area.

The evening turned to night and the searchers seemed more and more exhausted as he watched them return from each search. The hall's small kitchen was utilised and at three in the morning Macleod made good use of the instant coffee available. As he drank his fill, he watched the senior coastguard officer take a call on the radio. Hope was beside the man and after he had spoken to her briefly, she waved Macleod over.

'There's a small yacht out in the bay to the west, anchored just a little off shore,' said the coastguard officer. 'A local resident says he saw four women get into a tender and sail out to it at about eleven o'clock. It was dark but he had been walking his dog and as he passed the girls he heard English, and foreign accents, as he puts it.'

'You said the yacht was anchored out, can we get a vessel to it?'

'We are trying to get one from a local fisherman who one of our people knows. He's saying it should be ready in about half an hour.'

'I'll get down there. Hope, come with me. Can you keep the search going . . .?' Macleod sought a name but he did not have one for the man. Hope had dealt with the officer from the start and Macleod had only briefly heard the man's name.

'Hamish. Of course, we'll keep looking. By the way, if our guys go with you, it'll be for your own safety cover. Given the fact you've told us not to approach these people, I don't want my people to step onto that yacht.'

'Of course not, Hamish,' said Macleod. 'You've done a super job—just keep the search going in case this is a dead end.'

It was ten minutes to the small jetty where the fisherman's vessel was. It was only a small creel boat but it was ample to take Macleod, Hope and three other officers over to the yacht. As they pulled alongside, the fisherman tied up to the other vessel and Hope climbed on board the yacht. She pulled Macleod up as well and then rapped on one of the portholes. There came no reply and she banged again, harder.

'Okay,' came a voice from inside, 'I can bloody well hear you. Who the flaming hell is it? If that's those boys we saw earlier, there's no way you shits are getting in.' The accent was definitely English.

Hope stepped back as a small door opened and a woman who was indeed petite and brunette stepped out onto the deck. She was wearing only a dressing gown and looked shocked at the presence of Hope and Macleod.

'What the shit's this? Get off my yacht!'

'Police,' said Hope quietly, 'how many of you on board?'

'Police,' said the woman loudly, 'bloody police, Emma. What did you do? I didn't think you were that pissed.'

'How many on board?' asked Hope again but a little more firmly.

'Four,' said the girl. 'Me, my sister and Ingrid and her friend, Isla. They are in the other cabin. I think they're like partners. Good laugh anyway.'

The woman was clearly still drunk but Hope stepped forward and asked her to move to one side. On entering the cabin, Hope saw another woman in just a top who looked like the woman who opened the door. Behind Hope there were steps that led down to presumably another cabin. She heard Macleod following her and pointed down the steps, looking at the woman in the other cabin.

'Are they in there?' she asked. The woman nodded. Hope descended the small steps and then slid aside a door before her. The cabin was dark but Hope could see and smell enough. 'Get them out, sir, get them out of here quick.'

'If you need a light, you can work it from up here as well,' said an English voice.

The light in the cabin came on and Hope heard the woman behind her scream. There was blood in the tiny space, blood that covered the walls. And on the floor was a woman in her underwear. But her throat had been slashed. On the only bunk in the room was a rucksack which looked as if it had been ransacked. And on top of the ruck was a pair of thick-rimmed glasses.

Chapter 20

Hope was exhausted. After finding the body of the female traveller on the boat, they had started a search of the local area on foot, by boat, and by air but nothing had been found. Teams that had been out all night had continued or had been replaced and now, late in the evening, everyone was tired and sore. She felt like slipping under the sheets, maybe after a hot shower and lying there as Allinson did that thing where he manipulated her back.

She had never been one for massages and pampering but the way the man worked her muscles across her shoulders and then down to the small of her back was something else. When he had produced a bottle of oil she had been suspicious but afterwards she thought he would be perfect as a masseur if the budding friendship did not work out.

Macleod was in a small room at the rear of the community hall and fast asleep. She had checked on him only ten minutes previously after spending time earlier trying to convince him to sleep. Teams were standing down the search for the night and the man needed to rest. He had become grouchy, not a trait he usually bore, and it was affecting others who were also fatigued.

The theory was that Fiske had gone to ground, or at least

had gone off to the wilds, hiding out in Harris hills or had gone to the south of Harris amongst the rocky landscape that was hard to cover on foot. Hope believed she would still be following whatever leads she had about the location of the soldiers, despite having been wet from swimming off the boat that morning.

And that was the theory. Freja Fiske had seen or heard the search, spotted their interest in the boat she was on and made a swift departure. It was suspected she had intended to kill the other women on board too but the sisters had locked themselves into their cabin, a precaution that had saved their lives. Fiske would not have had a lot of time and so when she was confronted by the barred door, she had simply grabbed her gear and swam off across the sea loch in the dark.

Hope looked around the room before her and saw how empty it was compared to earlier in the day. Everyone was getting rest now that darkness had fallen and there were only a few uniformed officers who seemed to be active. Hope spoke to a sergeant and popped outside for air. Walking briskly to the harbour, she stood where the ferry berthed.

The night air was cool and she wondered where the woman was hiding. It would be perfectly possible to sleep outdoors but her clothes would still be damp. Unless she had acquired new clothes, which could mean . . . Hope did not want to think about more bodies. Thinking about Allinson's back rub was a more soothing thought as she took her break.

The road seemed to go on forever, endlessly rising and falling with crazy twists as you reached each peak. Just who had built this single-track road out to Scarp? Of course, he knew of the island, its history with rocket post but he had not been out this way to Hushinish beach for a long time. Usually he was based up at Stornoway and rarely got down this far but with all that was going on he had been sent to help with the searches.

Beside him was Sergeant Denny, a long-time veteran of the force who he had been a little afraid of since his arrival on Lewis. Manpower was stretched and advice was that no one should be out alone with the criminal they were looking for, so he had been assigned the Sergeant with him, as he, PC Davidson, was one of the rawest constables at the station.

This was an additional patrol along the roads in the area, seen as necessary due to the killing earlier in the morning, to assist in protecting the public and in case anything could be spotted despite it now being dark. They were to search along the road out to Hushinish beach and then return to the temporary base at Tarbet for a bit of sustenance. Davidson was looking forward to that food.

The lights of the vehicle he was driving struggled to illuminate the road as he crested another small but brutal summit on the road. It would rise maybe twenty feet before descending, but at the peak the road would swing left or right and until you started descending you did not see where the black tarmac was going. At this hour it was requiring his full concentration. He imagined that in the small hours of the morning it would require even more diligence.

They had stopped at a few small buildings and sheds on the road out, each fixture somehow carved into the rugged terrain, like someone had simply decided a house should be there, slap on the side of a steep slope or in the middle of a boggy dip of land. Out here in the wilds, as he called it, he wondered how people existed. Davidson had a flat in Stornoway and held onto it as the last bastion of sensible living. His adaptation to the island and its ways, which were so very different from that of Dundee, his home, was not going that smoothly. Only two weeks until leave, he thought. That's if we're not still driving down insane roads looking for this mad woman.

Hushinish beach suddenly appeared over the crest of a hill and as he continued on the small road past a few buildings, along the side of a hill, he thought he caught something in the moonlight.

'Sarge, can you see something on the beach?'

Beside him, Denny rolled her neck and stared out of the car window. 'Bloody hell, tourists. I mean that sea's freezing. And with all that's going on would you go skinny dipping?'

Davidson could see a single camper van in the car park beside the glass-fronted structure of the facilities block at Hushinish.It was one of the older types, but the people on the beach were certainly not older. He counted four of them and in the moonlight, he could see they were unclothed and running in and out of the small surf that was breaking onto the beach. In a lot of ways, the scene looked idyllic but given recent circumstances the people must be insane. Just about every other tourist had stayed away from this road and the area around the boat. The police had advised everyone to stay indoors and keep their homes locked. But here were a group of young people, happily acting like nothing was happening.

'Pull up to the car park and we shall go and have a word, Davidson. See if we can't persuade them to move away to a better site.'

The young constable parked the car and together the pair stepped across from the tarmac of the car park to the drop onto the beach and the lively bathing foursome. As the bathers spotted the police officers, Davidson expected then to be somewhat shamed and to start covering up their bodies but none of the four flinched, instead simply walking over to the officers.

'I'm sorry, folks,' said the sergeant, 'but I'm going to have to ask you to move on to another site quite far from here.'

The nearest man looked round at his friends, bewildered and then started waving with his hands and speaking in a language the sergeant had never heard.

'Crap, Davidson, bloody foreign tourists. Do you know what they're saying?'

'No, Sarge, not a word.'

'Do you think they could get some clothes on? How do you say get dressed in French or German?'

'Clothez-vous?'

'Shut up, Davidson. Right, let's take the bull by the horns.' The sergeant was aware that that might not have been the best of catchphrases to have chosen but she ignored Davidson's smirk and pointed the man to his vehicle before pretending to pull on a pair of trousers. The man nodded profusely and then called over to the rest of the party who made their way to the camper van. 'Let's see if they have a map and we can point out where to go. Anything to get them out of here, Davidson. Not a good idea to be about with that nutter on the loose.'

Davidson nodded and then walked back to the car park with his senior officer. On the way, he saw something through the large glass windows at the front of the amenities building. He could not be completely sure but he thought he saw someone move, a figure in the dark of the room, caught out by the moonlight shining through.

'Sarge, there's someone in that building.'

'Are you shitting me, Davidson?'

'No, I saw a figure.'

'Okay, first we keep walking nice and calmly, until we get to the car. We get the foreigners to go inside their vehicle and lock the door. Then we make a search of that building, but a safe one. We go together covering each other the whole way. You understand?' Davidson nodded. 'Keep speaking normally to me, Davidson; otherwise, they'll know we know and that's the last thing we want.'

'Sorry, Sarge.'

Sergeant Denny rolled her neck as they reached the vehicles and gently pushed the naked foreigners into their vehicle to get changed. She pointed at the locks on the car and waited until they were activated before trying a door. With the public locked up inside their camper van, Denny motioned for Davidson to follow her. Cautiously they approached the side door which was through a wire-fenced gate at the side of the car park.

'Stand behind me and follow me a few feet behind, Davidson. And have your stick ready.'

Denny opened the door by sliding it back. It made too much noise for her liking but she turned on her torch to light up the corridor ahead. There was no one there, just a long corridor that she could see contained a number of doors. Slowly, she crept up the corridor and opened the first door on her right. It was a woman's toilet and she was relieved to see the facility was empty. A second door further on was again inspected and nothing found, it being just another unoccupied toilet.

As she moved further along, she was aware there were large rooms on the left-hand side and that the doors were rolled back. The torchlight lit up the interior of one room and when there was no reaction inside, she stepped into the large room. Denny had been many years in the force and now all her experience meant that she was able to react and throw her hands up before the knife that was descending towards her head. As something cut across her cheek, she screamed.

Chapter 21

Davidson saw his colleague recoil, clutching her face, and turn away from the room entrance. As he moved towards her aid, a hand shot out from the room, grabbing Denny by the hair. As much in instinct as in sort of reaction to previous training, Davidson grabbed the handle of the slide door and pushed it closed. A second hand holding a knife had emerged and both arms were caught by the door closing, causing the knife to be dropped.

Instead of releasing the door, he pushed as hard as he could, keeping it closed on the white arms that were protruding. Whoever was inside was struggling to release the closing and he was unsure if his colleague was in a state of mind to react.

'Sarge! Sarge, are you okay?'

'No,' yelled Denny. 'God, look at the blood. Davidson, the blood.'

'Get out! Get to the car.'

'What about you?'

'I'm following, Sarge, but get on the radio and get out—get the foreigners out too. I'll hold here as long as I can.'

Denny did not hesitate and clutching her face, she stumbled along the hallway, back to the car park. Once through the fenced gate, she made for the camper van banging on the side door as hard as she could. It pulled back and the young man from the beach looked at her. Blood dripped on the interior of the van and he started shouting at Denny.

'Drive, you moron; get in the front and drive!'

The man continued to remonstrate but Denny had no time for this. 'Where's the keys? Where's the bloody keys!' The man looked at her, shocked but also in anger at his van becoming a temporary triage centre. Denny ignored him, scanning the inside of the van for the keys to start the engine, then gave up and opened the front door of the van and climbed into the front seat. Using her free hand, she activated her radio but no one responded when she called. *Bloody blackspot,* she thought and reached down to find the keys still in the ignition.

'Close the bastard door,' she yelled into the rear and a head popped up beside her. She pointed with her free hand at the door and started the engine. Her other hand could feel the blood pouring across it and she pressed harder. In normal times she would look for some sort of padding to place on top of the wound but she had to get away, and get these ignorant but innocent tourists out of here too. Davidson would just have to manage.

With one hand, she stretched across herself to place the van in gear and then as the van accelerated, she reached back and turned the wheel. It was awkward but it was a process she would repeat twice in the next ten seconds as she got the vehicle moving. As she pulled out of the car park and back along the single-track road, she pressed hard on the horn, just so Davidson would know she was clear; she hoped he was all right.

Inside the small building, Davidson was pushing hard against the door and could still see the arms trapped by the effort. But he was tiring as the person on the other side seemed to be growing stronger and started gaining ground. With one foot, he kicked out at the knife that had dropped and booted it down the hallway as hard as he could. It disappeared in the dark, much to his satisfaction.

He would have to make a run for it and now that Denny was clear, all he had to think about was himself. He'd get to the car, lock it down and then drive. After that the cavalry could come and get this nutter. As he leaned forward with his pressing action, his head became adjacent to a small glass rectangular window and he inadvertently looked through. Two eyes of fire looked back and he saw a snarl of determination. As he reared back, he saw a mop of blonde hair and pale skin under it. Under normal circumstances the woman would have looked quite attractive, maybe even very much so, but now, she looked like hell unleashed with her wild eyes.

He counted to himself, one, two, three, and go! Releasing the door, he turned and ran from the hallway as hard as he could. He could hear footsteps behind him and as he opened the fenced gate to the car park, he heard her burst out of the hallway.

She must have hurdled the gate for she caught him halfway across the car park, wrapping her arms around his legs and causing him to fall. He managed to roll after falling but she was on top. Davidson managed to grab one of her arms but he was punched hard in the face. He sought to block her but he was now struggling to make his body do what his brain told it and he received more blows. His hands sought some sort of purchase and he grabbed her hip, his fingers finding a belt, and with a move that was desperate in the extreme, he rolled and pulled the belt, managing to throw her off to the side.

She seemed shocked but he struggled to follow up on his success and instead rolled away towards the car. As she got to her feet and ran at him from behind, Davidson had a moment of clarity and calmly stepped to one side, grabbing her head and using her momentum to run her straight into the car door.

The thud rang out and she reeled backwards. In the moonlight, he saw her bleeding but used the chance to open the door and climb in. He locked the doors and started the engine. As he went to drive away a figure launched itself onto the bonnet of the car and he could not see anywhere ahead of him. There was a sickening crunch as the car hit something solid. The figure was flung off the car and he lost sight of her as the air bag deployed.

Hope tore along in the car with a waking Macleod beside her. When the call had come in, she had not hesitated, grabbing her boss from his makeshift bed and dragging him into the car. Racing through the night, she had turned on the emergency vehicle blue lights and was on the road to Hushinish beach in under ten minutes. The road itself was long and unyielding, single track for the most part and had curves that would make a rally car driver sweat.

Macleod was now fully awake beside her and calling on the radio for more back-up and for a helicopter to get airborne to assist. The terrain around them was a series of craggy hills covered with heather, peat bog, and turf. Any pursuit would be assisted to a large extent by an aerial asset.

They drove in silence apart from Macleod's organising of the officers to arrive behind them. An ambulance had been called for Sergeant Denny who had cut off her call suddenly. There was a sick feeling in Macleod's stomach and once again he felt behind the drag curve with this suspect. As they approached another of the small crests on the road, the headlights sending their beam off to the night sky, Macleod saw something on his left.

'Stop!'

Hope pressed the brakes hard bringing the car to a complete stop. Macleod was quickly out of the door and stomping through a boggy patch of land to a camper van that was sitting on its side. He ran to the front and saw the cracked glass of the windscreen. A female officer was sitting in the driver's seat, her hand covering her face and neck, with blood all around her.

'Get the medical kit, McGrath.' Using a small mound of turf, he jumped up onto the van and pulled open the passenger door. Macleod climbed inside and unclipped the seat belt of the officer whose eyes were gaunt as they stared at him.

'Denny? Are you Denny?' asked Macleod. There was a nod and Hope then appeared at the open passenger door above him. 'Can you move?'

'I'm mobile, I don't think anything is broken,' said the officer with a shaky voice. 'But Davidson is still back there. She's there with him; get him help.'

Hope was dropping a large compress to Macleod who removed the officer's hand from her face and examined the wound. There was a lot of blood but he could not see anything more untoward than a deep cut. He slapped the compress on the wound and then placed Denny's hand over it. In the distance, he heard sirens.

Hope had stepped down off the van and made her way to the rear where she opened the doors. Inside she saw a mess of clothing and fixtures and a host of legs. A man was lying moaning with a towel wrapped around him but with his genitalia exposed as the towel had ridden past his waist and onto his chest. He then sat up and began shouting in a language Hope did not understand. Beside him, a woman in a shirt and bare legs also started shouting.

A marked police car pulled up and two officers stepped out. 'Good,' said Hope and then waved them over. 'One officer down in the front needing medical assistance. Some foreigners in the rear, at least two who seem to only have minor injuries but they don't seem to speak English. There may be more. We're going to the visitor centre at Hushinish, one officer there, possibly down; send more our way as you can.'

With that Hope was off to the car, shouting Macleod to follow. She stepped into the vehicle, turned on the engine and then flung open the passenger door for Macleod. Before he had sat down the car was already pulling away and he desperately swung his door closed.

'When we get there, stay close Hope. This girl is serious work, so no heroics. Understood!'

Hope nodded but her mind was on the difficult road ahead. She had never been into cars and driving but had completed her advanced driving with the force, and now everything she had learnt was coming into play. She clipped the edge of the road at least twice and then almost spun off completely before they saw the blue lights of a police car in the visitor centre car park.

'Go beside the car and we'll spread out from there if the officer's not there,' said Macleod.

Hope threw the car into the car park and pulled up alongside the marked car which had an enormous dent in the front.

Macleod stepped out but could not see anyone in the car. He looked around in the darkness but could only hear the waves crashing. Except for the pollution of their lights, the scene was lit by only moonlight and seemed quiet beyond the damaged car.

'We'll check the centre first,' said Macleod, 'but lock the car.'

He heard the beeps and the locks dropping and walked over to the fenced gate. There was blood on the ground, a lot of it but it ended in the middle of the car park, not at the police car. He nodded at Hope to enter the centre via the open doorway.

Inside was dark and Hope took out her torch, shining it along the hallway. There was nothing but blood. A trail led from an open door along the hallway back to the car park. Carefully, Hope opened each door in the building, but found only toilets and empty rooms. Retreating outside, she asked her boss how to proceed.

'If she's here, she could be behind any number of hillocks or rocks, or she could be on the beach. Or maybe she has run and is back behind us in the hills. There're also some buildings back there and some more beyond. And where is our officer? If she killed him, why bother to hide him? We'll check the beach and then route along to the houses beyond the hall. Our officer might be hiding out, maybe injured.'

Together, they walked down to the wall that dropped down to the beach and began to sweep it, looking behind numerous large rocks at one end before walking to the far side, beyond the hall. As they swept the torches back and forth, a faint cry came on the wind.

'Help, she's here. She's close but I couldn't say anything in case she got to me before you.'

Macleod stepped to his right and looked behind a large rock.

A huddled officer was shaking as he sat on the ground.

'Dear God, thank you.'

He was sniffing, fighting back tears of relief, and shaking like he had a fever. Macleod kept him sitting exactly where he was while Hope checked the immediate area for the girl. When she found no one, Macleod pulled the man up to his feet and checked him for injuries but he could only find a few scratches although the uniform was drenched in sweat.

'Okay, officer, can you make it back to the car? I'll give you the keys and you can lock yourself in.'

'No . . . no . . . I'm not doing that, need someone with me. I was . . . in the car . . . last time.'

'What's your name, constable?' asked Macleod.

'Davidson, sir.' The formality seemed to bring a calming effect to Davidson but he was far from being in control of his emotions.

'McGrath, we need to get Davidson back to the car and wait for backup.'

'I'll go alone and search this bit, sir,' said Hope. 'She could get away.'

'No! We go back.'

'But she'll get away, sir.' Hope was becoming angry and started to move away from Macleod.

'I said no, McGrath. She's a killer and very proficient one. We stay safe and wait for back up. No one does this alone.'

Macleod took Davidson and led him back to the car park, followed by Hope who walked backwards most of the way, trying to keep her eyes on the darkness around them and the area beyond where they had searched. As they got to the car, the first marked car arrived and Macleod quickly ordered one of the officers to follow him and deposited Davidson in the car.

Hope was some fifty metres ahead of Macleod, racing back up to where they had found Davidson. There were more rocks to search but beyond that the ground turned back to tightly woven grass and sand with a road running beyond to some houses. They were all dark and Macleod was not relishing this search.

'Stay close, McGrath,' he ordered. The other officer was searching the rocks closer to the water while Hope covered those nearer to the road. She was drifting off, gradually getting further away from Macleod. He checked the officer on his seaward side again and then heard Hope grunt.

Someone had grabbed her from behind and had arms around her throat, like they were going to snap her neck. But the hold was awkward as they were on tip toe due to Hope's height and whilst she was struggling, she had managed to lift her attacker off her feet.

Macleod raced over rocks and then slipped crashing to the ground and cutting his knee of a sharp rock. The other officer came hurtling past and threw himself at Hope's attacker, taking everyone to the ground. Macleod could not see them as the party of three descended behind the rocks but he heard Hope begin to cough.

Scrambling back to his feet, Macleod began to run to the melee. He saw the officer stand up and face the attacker before the woman delivered several punches to the chest and then a couple to the head. The man fell, knocked out by the look of it. Macleod approached and saw Hope still choking on the ground.

'I'm right here,' yelled Macleod at the woman, 'right before you. That's it, come get me.' Macleod was not feeling brave but rather scared. But he had to draw attention from McGrath in her prone position. He knew he was no fighter compared to McGrath or this woman. They had youth on their side and bodies that could throw a decent punch so he needed to use some guile if he was walking away from this one.

'Who is it that you're going for? I know you want to kill them. I know about your mother's time in the army.' There was nothing but eyes focused on him and the woman moved closer. 'I know Malthe Amundsen helped her come here. I know you have a sister.' And there was a slight moment of recognition. 'I want her to be safe too. Tell me where to go and I'll go right in and pluck her out. I'll send the others to jail. Tell me where I need to look.' Macleod held up his hands, leaving himself exposed. 'Let me find her. Trust me.' For a moment he thought he saw some recognition in the woman's eyes, a possible softening. But the rage returned and he knew he was in trouble.

Seeing a shadow behind the girl, Macleod realised that Hope had moved. He held his hands up as the woman advanced feigning that he would not fight back. This drew her closer, more quickly. As she reached him, he heard a yell and the woman fell into him as she was kicked hard in the back. Macleod fell to the ground and the pale face of Freja Fiske was pressed up against his. But she was pulled back up as Hope tried to snap handcuffs on her wrists as she pulled the woman's arms behind her.

There was a struggle before Freja pulled an arm free and lashed at Hope with it, knocking her backwards. Macleod was taken aback by the ferocity, something he was well used to encountering but this was in an abundance and to a level he had rarely seen. As Freja reached for Hope, Macleod ran and drove his shoulder at the small woman knocking her off her feet. They crashed into rocks, Macleod hitting his legs hard on them.

Freja was up before Macleod but Hope had engaged her and Macleod saw them trading blows before Freja caught Hope with a fist to the jaw that must have hurt badly. Hope fell backwards but much to Macleod's relief, Fiske simply ran off. It was then he heard more sirens and saw flashing lights coming along the road.

Hope was back on her feet and running hard after Fiske who disappeared towards the houses they had seen earlier. There was only moonlight here and Macleod saw Hope round the corner of a house. He raced after her and heard a yell before he turned the same corner. The women were in a clinch with Hope losing it badly. Fiske had her hands on Hope's throat, throttling her, while Hope was trying to knock her opponent's arms down to break the hold.

Macleod was not sure he had been seen and so quickly took off his coat and walked quickly but quietly behind Fiske at a distance. He heard Hope's choked cries but kept his discipline until he was entirely behind Fiske and then approached. He prayed he would not hit any wayward stone or piece of ground to give away his presence and then opened the coat and quickly wrapped it over Fiske's head. With the element of surprise, he kicked hard on the back of the woman's knees dropping her to the ground.

She let go of Hope but her arms were up and pulling the coat off her head. As Macleod made a grab for her, she rolled forward before turning to face him.

'I can get her to safety; tell me where she is! Please!'

Fiske stared at him and for a moment, the panic of battle

had settled and the sound of the crashing waves took over once more. There was a shake of the head. 'Mother said they needed to pay. There will be no jail, no reprieve for them. They destroyed my mother and now they destroy my sister over and over again. Malthe was meant to look after her, find her a home. He only gave her a hell.'

Shouts and yells could now be heard and Macleod knew his backup was now arriving in force. 'I will find them,' said Fiske, 'and I will give you the girls to look after. But they will pay for what they did to my family. Keep out of my way, policeman.'

Macleod went to step forward and offer more to keep her talking but she turned away, running towards the sea behind the houses. Hope was on her feet and managed to grab the woman's arm but received a blow to the face for her troubles. In the darkness, Macleod saw the shape of a small boat, an outboard engine on the back. He gave chase but his legs were giving out now after their battering on the rocks.

As he arrived at the beach, he saw Fiske start the motor and push the boat out into the surf. Soon she was just the sound of an engine in the dark and Macleod dropped to his knees. *Dammit, so close.* Turning back to Hope, he saw her staggering towards him. 'You okay?' he asked.

'No,' she said and knelt down beside him. 'She nearly killed me—she nearly had me, Seoras.'

There was a tremble in Hope's voice that was not normal and she leaned in on Macleod's shoulder. 'But she didn't. I'm so very glad she didn't.'

Chapter 22

The weather had changed dramatically in less than a day. Thick, low, grey clouds had spread over the islands like an enormous duvet and drizzle had begun to cast a damp mood on an investigation that was already frustrating. Macleod was livid with himself for letting Fiske get away and yet he also recognised he was within an inch of having lost his partner's life. A lack of sleep and case fatigue made him storm around the temporary base in Tarbet like the proverbial bear with a sore head, but one in a bad mood as well.

The medics had checked Hope over and asked her to go to the hospital for further treatment when able and Macleod had told her now was as good a time as any. But with a stubbornness he had become used to, she had remained despite the severe bruising on her neck. The mark had developed rapidly and was a deep purple giving her a bizarre scarf under her blouse collar.

The inclement weather had made helicopter operations difficult and a haar—the thick, sea-originating fog—was starting to form on the inlets around Harris, meaning visibility was at a premium. The local searches continued with uniformed officers stopping residents and tourists alike as they travelled about, asking if they had seen anything unusual. Most returned a negative but two pieces of information landed on Macleod's desk as the day began to fade into darkness less than twenty-four hours after the incident at Hushinish.

'Leverburgh, she was sighted in Leverburgh, Hope. Less than six hours ago. Not just once but six times.'

'She must be getting tired and hungry. They said one of the places she was seen was in the local shop. The CCTV picture should be with us in a few minutes but I've pulled together assets for a search in the area. I'm trying to cross reference where she was seen with where we have had reports of mini-buses or vans. There was also that boat from Ullapool in that area.' Hope reached up and felt her neck before continuing. 'What was the other sighting?'

'On the road that runs along the east side of Harris, it's a bloody awful road that swings up and down and should be in the World Rally championship, not on a tourist route. But we have had no other sightings there. And time wise, it seems a bit much for her to have been in both areas. The sighting on the east side was between other sightings.' Macleod stood with his hands on the desk in front of him.

'What's up?' asked Hope.

'What do you make of these sightings in Leverburgh? It's all a bit sudden. We have struggled to trace her, it's all been a tip off here and there, a random sighting, and even then, we have been behind the drag curve. But now we have as definite a sighting as you could hope from someone on the run. Feels too easy, Hope.'

'You're just tired, sir. And so is she. She's slipping. She might have taken a bit out of me last night but I also took something from her too. She's gone for food and a bit of respite but she's left the Tarbet area to do it.'

She looked at Macleod with eyes that said he was wrong and that they should just get on with it. Maybe she was right but something was nagging at him. If there had been just something more concrete.

He sat back down and sipped on his coffee. Why was it that images and statements and everything that could confirm things always arrived later than you wanted? He watched Hope calling colleagues on the radio and organising search teams to cover Leverburgh. She was keen as ever but she was also looking jaded. And with good reason. But this was the dangerous time. This was when you missed something; experience had taught him that. Hope still had that confidence of younger days that eluded him now but what he had in return was a questioning mind, even when things seemed bang to rights.

An image was thrust in front of him. 'CCTV image, sir. That's Fiske all right, in the local shop. The other sightings give her as being between there and the ferry terminal. We've checked with the crew of the Leverburgh ferry, which was not easy as it docks for the night on the other island. They don't remember seeing anyone like her.'

Macleod nodded. 'She's not gone off the island, Hope. She'll make a statement when she catches up with the soldiers. Are the search teams deployed yet? And they know not to engage?'

'All done, sir. They are in Leverburgh and spreading out now.'

'Good, keep me advised.'

After an hour, Macleod stepped outside for a moment of fresh air to blow away the cobwebs in his mind. The coastal path on the east side kept coming back to his mind.

She was even about half way along it. There were so many little hideouts along there, houses that people just passed by because you would not drive that road unless you had to, or were tourists looking at the moon-like features of the rocky landscape on that side.

Leverburgh was wrong for a place to run some sort of secret brothel. Although it was by no means a large village, it was the largest place in the area. The coast road was more discreet. You could also land a craft at night without being seen. In Leverburgh, the harbour had too many eyes. Better to use a discrete cove, bring your clients in off a boat that was always seen, like pleasure cruises from the mainland, coming that way often and then dropping people off at night to the brothel they were running.

Now I'm thinking like she would. Now I'm in the right mindset. All you would have to do is sit and watch for that vessel. If you had the right area. Maybe she knew how but not the location and she's working her way round them all. But now she's got us on her tail. Maybe . . .

Macleod's contemplations were cut short as Hope burst out of the doors, running up to him. 'We have her trapped. She's holed up with a family, has them at knifepoint. I'm getting the car.' And with that Hope was off and Macleod's mind was scrambling from his previous thoughts to the situation at hand. He ran inside to grab his jacket and then outside to join Hope in the car.

They raced along awkward roads to Leverburgh but the journey was slow and took a half hour before they arrived in the village. It was located in a flat part of the land at the end of hills and was grouped around the ferry terminal which opened up into the sound of Harris, a treacherous patch of water between North Uist and the Isle of Harris. There were some lights on in the village but Macleod could see where they were heading by a circus of light consisting of flashing blues and white headlights.

As they pulled up in front of a small detached building, a sergeant intercepted. 'Sir, she's inside holding a knife to the throat of a child. She's communicating only through the father, a Mr Donald MacIver, who is talking to us from the hall. The front door is locked according to the father and we are at a distance as per your instruction not to engage.'

Macleod looked at the brightly lit building before him. 'How many in the house?'

'Just the father, mother, child, and our suspect.'

'Has she made any demands?'

'Not yet, sir, I think we caught her unawares. The father shouted through the door at the search team as they approached the house,' said the sergeant.

'And they were doing what at the house at the time?'

'Just a basic search around the gardens, checking walls and the like, the standard searches in case she was hiding anywhere in the garden. There is a lot of cover in that garden and they were sweeping it with their torches when the father called out.'

Macleod was not happy, something did not feel right. 'Have we seen our suspect?'

'Only the father has been seen through the small glass pane in the door. But we have heard the mother crying, sir, screaming at times for her boy.'

'Do we know the age of the child?' asked Hope.

'Just a year.'

'Thank you, Sergeant, keep everyone at the perimeter for now. No one goes close until I say so.'

Macleod stood at the low wall that surrounded the grounds of the house. It was in full view of at least another eight houses and to walk to it would have involved walking past another twenty houses at least coming from the village centre.

'How do we play it?' asked Hope.

'We don't rush and we talk to the father. We negotiate and if necessary we will eventually storm the building if we think the child is in immediate danger. Get a team ready who can do that, please, McGrath.'

Hope turned away and Macleod was left standing alone, looking at the house. *Why has she trapped herself in there? She has never been caught out by us. At Hushinish, she was stumbled upon but she reacted and got out. She was aggressive, no negotiations. On the small boat at Tarbet, she was again aggressive, sorted her problems before we were even in place. She came out to me and PC Ross when we had her trapped. This is wrong, not how she would react. But there's a kid involved, so I need to be sure. Damn.*

Macleod looked for Hope and called her over. 'I'm going to go to the front door and talk to the father. I want you to go around the back onto the beach and approach the house from the rear. Get up close to the window and see if you can see inside. I want a positive identification on our suspect.'

'Is that wise, sir? She might see me coming and harm them.'

'Then get the squad you have assembled ready to go. We'll use them if it goes south.'

'Goes south,' said Hope, barely containing her anger, 'this is crazy. What are you doing? This is not the way we handle these things.'

'Hope,' said Macleod, 'this is all wrong. How did she get herself trapped in there? Look at this place, she's on the run for goodness sake and she picks somewhere she knows we'll be. She's sighted like wildfire after being so elusive; it's ridiculous. This is a ruse, a way of keeping us out of the way while she hunts down her prey.'

'Well that's a good theory and you might be right but you are gambling on your intuition. There's a baby in there who doesn't need those odds. We can't play it like this.'

'We have to. If we don't, they'll be a blood bath in that house where the soldiers are.'

'And if you are wrong there'll be one right here. Seoras, you can't do this on a hunch.'

'It's stronger than that.'

'And what's to stop us just going looking for her, elsewhere and leaving this situation like this.' Hope was standing up to her full height and Macleod felt small beneath her. But he was right—he had to be.

'Because we need to know what the parents in there know to find her. And if we wait, then she'll kill the others.'

'I think it's too great a risk.'

'Noted,' said Macleod, 'but we go. Now get round to the rear of that building and approach it in three minutes. Stay low and no unnecessary risks.'

'I think you're the one taking the unnecessary risks.' Hope stormed off but Macleod watched her walk away from the scene and then casually make her way down to the beach behind the house. He advised the sergeant he was making an approach to the front door and strode up the steps and called through to the father inside.

'Donald, this is DI Macleod. I'm just going to sit here and talk to you. Are you all still okay?'

'Yes,' came a quick response, 'but she has our Iain. She's got

Iain; don't do anything.'

'It's okay, Donald. I'm just sitting on the step talking to you.' Macleod sat down on the step and found it cold. But he was making sure he did not look like a threat, just in case he was wrong. 'Can you ask Freja what it is she wants?'

'No,' came a quick reply, 'I can't. She told me to stay out here and not ask questions.'

'But how do we know if your family is still safe?'

'She said they would be if I stayed here and told you to just stay out there. She doesn't want to talk.'

Macleod thought about his next words. He did not want to be too aggressive but he needed to know what was happening inside. 'Can we get you all some food? Maybe you could open the door and get some food. It will be a long night otherwise. Ask Freja for me, Donald.'

'I can't!'

'She's in the next room, isn't she? I'm sure she'll hear you.'

'I can't!' screamed the man. 'She'll kill them.'

'For asking a question. I doubt it because she's surrounded and needs to get out. You can ask her, Donald. If you don't, I'll have to ask her.'

Macleod could hear panic in the hallway beyond the door. Donald was whispering to someone. Macleod looked back to the array of cars and people outside the garden wall and saw Hope standing front and centre. He mouthed a word to her and she shook her head. She had not sighted their suspect.

'Well, Donald, did you ask her? I heard you whispering.'

'No, I wasn't.'

'Well ask her, because if you don't I will. In fact, I'm coming in.'

The man was suddenly at the window pane. In a hushed

voice, he quickly said, 'Don't. She's got my Iain. I'll tell you everything but for God's sake don't open the door. She'll kill him. I'm sure she's watching; she said she'll be watching.'

Chapter 23

Macleod tried to act as if nothing had changed and sat down on the step of the house with his face to the door. It had all just become a lot more complicated and he needed to think how to do this. But he needed more information. He could see now why she had chosen this house. With a pair of binoculars, you could see it for miles from up in the hills. She might have this child with her and could carry out the threat she had made. More than likely though, she had stashed the child somewhere while she carried out her actions against the soldiers, if she knew where they were. But she must know; otherwise, why carry out this action?

'Stay calm, sir, I'm not opening the door.is threatmeably a child why she had chosen this house. But you need to talk to me, okay?' Macleod hoped he sounded commanding and was aware of the safety of the child. 'Did she take anything when she left the house?'

'Yes, I think she took the car keys. Iain has a car seat, she kept asking if the car had a car seat in it.'

'And your car, sir, describe it, please.'

'Red, deep red, old style Vauxhall Astra hatchback.' He gave the licence plate but Macleod had to get him to repeat it five times before the man stopped jumbling the numbers and letters.

'Good, and did she go off in any particular direction?'

'Towards Rodel way. I could just about see her. She didn't go towards the shop, I watched that closely so she must have gone to Rodel. You need to get Iain; my wife is a mess—she's not speaking now. I think she has collapsed.'

'Okay, you can go to her in a minute,' said Macleod, needing more details before the man went further inside the house and became hard to talk to.

'But she's collapsed.'

'What was the woman wearing?'

'Black, everything was black. She took my wife's things. We had been out walking with Iain in the pram and she joined us as we were coming into the house. She put a knife to my back and got us inside. I need to go, Chris-Anne is in a mess.' The man sounded close to breakdown, and no wonder with his child missing in the grasp of a killer. The press had told the story of the previous killing on the boat and his own people had released a statement for everyone to stay indoors. People never listen though.

Macleod stood up and calmly walked back to the exterior wall of the garden and was approached by Hope and the sergeant at the scene.

'She's got their baby and has claimed that she's watching the house. He's been told to tell us that Fiske is inside, and he said she's watching the house. Given the view around her, she could be halfway up that hill beside us and still see.'

'But why?' asked Hope. 'She's looking for the soldiers, so why bother with this charade.'

'Because we got so close last time. She's worried we'll stop her so she devises this. I mean, can we leave? Of course not, not with the child missing. So the bulk of our units need to stay; otherwise, she'll know that we know what Mr MacIver has told us and she might kill the child.'

'So, we keep the circus going here and send only a few cars away,' said Hope. 'Make it look like we bought it.'

'Yes, but only one car goes; we redirect others and they need to be unmarked. We can't have any blue lights scaring her into something stupid. Sergeant, find me an officer that looks like me.'

The sergeant looked at Macleod quizzically, before sizing him up and then disappearing into the melee behind him.

'We'll set up a decoy and then you and I will get in a car and head for Rodel,' said Macleod. 'And not the car we've been using in case she recognises it. Sort one while I change, McGrath. And also get on to anyone else we haven't just sent here, and if they have an unmarked car, send it on the road that routes down the east side of Harris. But tell them to space out. It's not a busy road and if we flood, it she'll know.'

Hope nodded but seemed to be deep in thought before asking, 'Are you sure she's on that side? It's not another ruse?'

'I'm sure of nothing, McGrath, but she's dressed in black and I reckon she's found her people. She's worried in case we have found them too so she set this up. I think she's going for it tonight. So, we need to find the family car, a deep red Vauxhall Astra hatchback and then see what buildings it is close to.'

Hope turned away and Macleod caught a worried face before she exited. His attention was grabbed by an officer who now stood in front of him. The man was younger but of a similar height, had Macleod's broad shoulders and sported dark hair. 'Excellent, I think you need my coat, constable.'

A few minutes later, Macleod had given the constable a change of jacket, instructions to keep going back and forward to the door every ten minutes or so and to pretend to have a serious conversation with whoever was inside. These actions were to continue until advised.

Now wearing a dark jacket marked 'Police' on its rear, Macleod found Hope and they departed the scene in a new unmarked car. Macleod let Hope drive as he wanted to scan the area, an area he knew better than Hope, having been brought up on the islands.

'There's so many little roads leading off to buildings near the shore once you get past Rodel. Bays you can sail into at night, houses almost hidden, it would be perfect to run their sex holiday business.'

Hope drove up the climb between a high mountain on one side and a small hill that obscured the sea towards Rodel. The darkness made it hard to see anything but the odd light in a house. But Macleod was convinced this was not the place due to the lack of access except from the road. They must be bringing their punters ashore in boats; it was the safest way.

They drove past Rodel church before swinging the car around to check the landing bay once used by royalty with its grass-covered concrete pier. There was nothing there and so they continued along the winding road that climbed and dropped more than a fairground ride. There was the occasional light from a house by the sea but nothing untoward. Macleod was becoming frustrated.

'Drive down the next turn off. It'll be an artist's studio or something but we need to start checking these houses. Anything with a van would be good. They spent the next hour checking every small road that led to the shore but none of the houses there gave any cause for concern. There were no vans, nothing that looked out of the ordinary. Back on the crazy road that ran along the east coast, they had almost returned to Rodel church when Macleod looked up at the craggy hillside on their right. He saw a large aerial and an old, ruined building. It was small, more like a store or a unit to keep equipment. But he thought he saw something behind it in the shadows. It was just a glimpse but it was a straw to clutch.

'Hope, up the next track on the right.'

'I thought you said the coast was where it would be.'

'I did,' agreed Macleod, 'but I thought I saw something.'

The track that ran off the road was a rugged one, large stones forming its base and providing a bumpy ride as the car was swung around a large upward bend. At the rise there were two aerial sites, one was the large single mast reaching for the sky Macleod had seen from the road. Beyond it was the rectangular box-topped smaller mast of a mobile network.

Hope steered the car towards the larger mast and in the shadow of the run-down building they had seen was a red hatchback. It had been driven off the track and onto the lumpy turf so that it could be hidden and it looked to be bogged down. Scanning the number plate, Macleod recognised it as that of Mr Donald MacIver of Leverburgh. Fiske was, or had been, here.

'Careful,' said Macleod on exiting the vehicle.

'You don't need to say. My neck's still sore to touch,' said Hope.

Beside the large mast was a concrete building, smaller than the derelict one. It was a dirty white and had a wooden door one side. Macleod walked up to it and gently pushed the door. As the door swung open, he noted the smashed locking mechanism and stood back in case someone leapt out. When no one came, Macleod stepped inside. On his right-hand side, he saw a brush and an old plastic chair. Before him was an electrical cabinet with a number of racks of equipment, presumably to do with the mast. There were some lights which gave an eerie glow to the small room.

Stepping behind the rack, he saw a table with some files, many marked as a log of some kind. Then in the dark recess behind the racking, he kicked his foot on something solid. It moved, swinging back and forward in a rocking motion. As his eyes adjusted to the lack of light, Macleod bent down and drew face to face with a large baby, maybe one year old.

'I think I have the baby, Hope. Ring through and get another unmarked car up here to take him away. But tell them to go easy with the lights. She might still be around, but I doubt it.'

'Shall we put him in the car?' asked Hope.

'No, he's asleep. Let him be until the car gets here. Let's wait outside.'

Macleod took Hope to the edge of the small building and looked out into the Harris night, checking the land before them. 'No car with her, so it's here, in front of us, Hope. One of the houses down there is the one. But which?'

'Over there,' said Hope. 'Can you see the jetty?' Macleod could not but then his eyes were not that good over the very long distance. 'There's a jetty there, and look, Seoras, about a mile off there's a boat.'

'Could be any boat, all you can see are the lights.'

'True,' said Hope, 'but, you said a boat, a place to come ashore and then we need a house.'

'Yes,' said Macleod, 'but look at the houses down there, there's what, six of them. That's got to be the most populated area this side of Harris. You couldn't sneak around there in full view of your neighbours.'

Hope swore. 'But it's got to be here somewhere. That's the only jetty I can see.' The height they were at gave an excellent view and Macleod too could not see another jetty or pier where a boat could land. Maybe Fiske was just throwing them off course big style and she had legged it back to the other side of the island. In reality all he had was a theory. And then it clicked.

'Hope, what if they owned all of the houses? What if they don't have any neighbours?'

'Then it would be perfect,' said Hope as they saw the lights of a car sweep along the rocky climb up to their position. 'You could pretend that you were all strangers, maybe even have couples living there for real, running the show.'

Macleod began to run for the car as the other vehicle parked beside their own. 'The MacIver baby is in the white building asleep. Get him back to his parents and stand down around them. All units to route towards those houses down there,' said Macleod, pointing to the small group. 'Let's hope we are not too late.' With that he got into the car and was joined by Hope. She spun the car around and drove fast over the rocky descent, so quick that Macleod felt slightly sick, like he was being tossed about on a rough sea.

Once on the main road, Hope took the turnoff to the small group of houses, passing the small link road to the jetty she had seen. The buildings were not in a neat cul-de-sac but were lying higgledy-piggledy off the road. There was no movement, so Macleod told Hope to pull up at the first one.

The house looked dark and Macleod swept the exterior from one side while Hope came the other way. At a large window with its curtains drawn, Macleod stopped and listened. He could hear the grunts of a man, who urged some 'bitch' for more. He felt sick because he heard no joy in the voice but rather a dominance. When he met Hope at the rear of the building, he stepped up to the back door and found it unlocked. Were they really so brazen, so comfortable in their scheme that they thought they could just hide out in plain sight?

As he entered the kitchen through the door, a light came on and a slim, attractive woman of maybe forty, asked him if she could help.

'Police, step aside.'

He clocked the knife as soon as she pulled it from behind her back and Macleod drove her into a wall. The woman's head bounced off it and she fell to the floor, seemingly knocked out. Macleod strode on into the house which had a low light on in the interior hallway. He could still hear the cries of a man, relishing what sounded like a hell for the woman he was with. Then came a slap, a full-on brutal one, not some playful love tap that some fetishists might enjoy.

Macleod kicked open a door and a naked man turned around, telling him to 'Get the hell out, I paid for this one.'

'Police,' said Macleod and the man immediately reached for him. Macleod grabbed his arm and brought it up behind his back, applying handcuffs first to one wrist and then the other before forcing the man to his knees. Hope ran past him to a naked girl in the far corner of the room. She had a bruised face and recoiled from Hope's approach. Grabbing a sheet from the bed, Hope gently wrapped it over the girl, telling her it was okay. She lifted the girl's head and shouted to Macleod.

'Sir, from Amundsen's photograph. It's Fiske's girl.'

Chapter 24

'Stay with her,' said Macleod. 'Stay with her until the backup comes. I'm going to see if I can get to a few more. These guys might just kill these women if they think they might talk.'

'But you can't go on your own,' argued Hope. 'She's out there. If you arrest the soldiers, she might take you out to get to them.'

'I'm calling for backup to flood the place. They should already be on their way. Join me as soon as you can. I'll observe and only act if I need to.'

Hope looked at him as if his last line was the biggest lie he had ever told. And she was right. How was he going to observe only? As soon as he saw one of the girls in danger, he'd react. And Hope would too, in his place. Macleod grabbed his mobile and called his temporary base at Tarbet. Everyone was already redirecting but he told them to come in silent yet not to hang back. With that he smiled at Hope and retraced his steps to the outside of the house.

The other houses were as dark as this one and Macleod made his way to the house next to the first one they had entered. It was another average build, probably with three bedrooms. Keeping as quiet as he could, Macleod approached an outer wall of the house where there were no windows. He listened intently but heard nothing and then ran in a half crouch around the building until he found an entrance. The door was PVC and had a small window at the top. Macleod raised his head and peeked through the window. Inside was a dark hallway with atypical furniture of a house; the mirror on the wall, a small drawer unit with a telephone set on top and stairs leading up.

Macleod tried the handle of the door which gave way easily and the door opened. He tiptoed inside and again listened intently but there was only a single snore. After years on the force, Macleod had a step that belied his age and weight. He could step quietly anywhere and now in a house with carpet on the floor, he was walking almost without sound. He swept through the bottom of the house, entering a kitchen, a living room and a dining room but finding no one. Maybe this was an empty house. But he had heard a snore upstairs.

Macleod returned to the stairs and stole up them keeping close to the wall. About halfway up, the stairway creaked under his weight despite his running up the edge of it. Rather than freeze, Macleod kept climbing to the top of the stairs where he encountered a blind turn to what would presumably be a landing. It was here he halted trying to not breathe heavily.

It was as he was leaning forward, trying to gently suck back in the oxygen he had used up during his combing of the lower floor that he heard a creak on the landing. It was subtle, probably imperceptible amongst the sounds of daytime but here in the dark of the night, it could be picked up by a listening ear. Macleod dropped into a crouch.

The iron bar struck the wall above him causing plaster to fall off the wall onto Macleod's back. But rather than wait to see who it was, Macleod drove himself up into the figure's open mid-riff and pumped his legs until they ran into the wall beyond them. Together they fell in a heap but Macleod was ready for that fall and rose the quickest, throwing a punch into his attacker's face. He followed it with a second, and then a third before being satisfied that the man would not be coming back up in a hurry.

The face before him was male and not the prettiest he had seen. Behind him lay the iron bar that would have rearranged his own face. But the snoring had stopped, the gentle rhythmic rise and fall was gone. Macleod doubted it had belonged to the man at his feet and he looked along the hallway and saw three doors.

The first he opened contained a bathroom that was unlit. Beside it, the second door revealed a bedroom, made up with two single beds. The room was sparsely furnished and Macleod believed this was probably used for guard duty. Approaching the third door, he thought he heard some bed springs adjusting. He threw back the door and looked with horror at a woman lying on a bed before him. She was covered in bruises and was shaking at the sight of him. Beyond her was a double bed with four women on it as well as various mats on the floor.

Stepping forward, Macleod watched the woman before him throw her hands up to her face, protecting herself as the other women coiled away. They aged from late teens to at least their fifties if not more. He saw a blonde woman who looked around Jane's age, standing bare against the wall at the rear of the bedroom. All of them were terrified at the sight of him.

'Police,' said Macleod; 'it's okay, I'm with the police.' There was little comprehension and the women just backed away. 'Police, gendarmerie, poliezei, policia.' Macleod was no linguist but you learnt a bit of on the force. However, he was at his limit with the major European languages. Rather than step into the room, which he believed would cause terror and panic, he simply said, 'It's okay, it'll be okay, I'm police.' With that, he closed the door.

Macleod felt sick to the core at what he had seen but collected his thoughts. He could not simply leave these women here, as he had a suspect on the floor. He would need backup now. He had wanted to catch Fiske before she went through the houses but he was now losing time. His feelings were awash but he knew he had to protect the women he had seen before moving on.

There was the sound of feet at the front door and Macleod edged to the corner of the landing where it met the stairs. Glancing round, he saw a uniformed officer making their way slowly up the stairs. The large man was followed by a female officer.

'Good, up here, both of you, this house is safe. Names, please.' Macleod had seen the officers about but he had not had time to find out everyone's name due to the numbers which had been on the hunt for their suspect.

'Mackenzie and that's Harris behind me, sir.' The officer was thick set and obviously one of the first in due to his size. His colleague was not small, in fact probably bigger than the average woman, but she was still dwarfed by the man, as was Macleod.

'Mackenzie, cuff this guy behind me and keep him quiet. Harris, behind the door over there is a group of very scared women who look like they have been abused for some time. Keep them safe, and keep them as calm as you can. Mackenzie, don't go in the room unless you have to. They are scared witless by men. I told them I was police and they still recoiled. Stay here and protect them until we secure the area and we can get them somewhere better.'

Macleod was descending the stairs before the word 'sir' had left the officers' mouths. As he exited the front door, he saw officers moving into other houses. There were three more he had not been in, one of which had a barn-sized building stretching out behind it. He saw Hope entering that building and followed her across to it. There were now officers everywhere.

On entering the large building, Macleod was greeted with the occasional 'sir' by officers taking away sheepish-looking men. As he entered the large barn section of the building, he saw the words 'Fantasyland' on a placard on the wall. Either side of the words were two women in highly sexualised poses.

The barn section consisted of two floors of individual rooms stylized to certain tastes. They were beyond Macleod's experience and he tried not to think about them but rather focus on the job at hand. As he quickly toured the various rooms, Hope emerged from one and called a female officer to her. Seeing Macleod, she waved him over as well.

Inside the room was an array of devices that seemed to give out pain. It was like a horror dungeon. A woman was huddled on the floor and the female officer was covering her up. Then Macleod looked across and saw a man nailed to the wall. Looking at him, Macleod felt the bile in his throat, but he also understood why. He was looking at Felix Nyman, or what was left of him. Macleod stepped out of the room and Hope followed once the female officer and the distressed woman had left.

'She really made him suffer,' said Hope quietly. 'And he

bloody deserved it.'

Macleod looked at the rooms around him, as his mind told him his Sunday school teaching from his early days. 'Every life is precious, Hope, every life. But yes, I don't like to say it but seeing all this, I might have gutted him myself.'

He saw Hope's shocked stare to which he simply shrugged his shoulders. What did she expect? These weren't men; they were animals, demons. He knew that God forgave but he would find it hard to. The image of the woman who was around Jane's age and how terrified she had been in seeing him at the door of the room was haunting him. *Come on, Seoras, the day's not done.*

'McGrath, outside, we need to account for our soldiers. We only have one.'

It took another ten minutes to collate what was happening and their two still surviving Danish soldiers were missing. There had been only six people running the operation in the houses but there were over twenty so-called guests and nearly thirty captive women. Three of the four operators of the facility were dead, killed quickly, not tortured like Nyman. Eight guests were dead, again killed quickly. But there was no sign of Fiske. She had come and gone.

'Where are our other two?' raged Macleod. They had missed Fiske and although the freeing of these abused women was a triumph he was delighted about, the trail of death had gone on long enough. Where would Fiske take it now?

'The boat that's off shore, sir? We need to get out to it. It's still sitting there.'

'Why is it still there? I mean, McGrath, they must have seen us now all over here. Even without the blues, we still have lights and all the activity.'

Macleod walked past the houses to look out to sea. He could see the lights from the vessel but struggled to make out its size and shape. It must be maybe a half a mile off shore. But Hope was right—they needed to check it. Even though his ideas about it were changing as it had not run, he knew that to tidy everything up they should just make sure it was not involved.

'I could swim that,' said Hope.

'We'll get a boat and go out,' said Macleod.

'I wasn't suggesting I strip off and swim out for a look, I'm saying, I could swim that. Maybe she could too. I mean that's what she really wants, these guys who destroyed her mother and now her half-sister. She didn't come to take her sister away with her; she came for them.'

'And when she doesn't find them, she thinks of the boat and swims out,' said Macleod.

'Or maybe she knows the vessel, maybe that was what she saw, same as we did. And if she knows they are here then she will think they are there.'

'And she'll want the same as she wanted for Nyman.' Macleod saw Nyman's body nailed to the wall. There had been mutilation of his exterior parts and his face had been a tapestry of agony. And yet as horrified as Macleod was by the image, he still struggled to find sympathy for him. For a split second, he even thought that they should leave Fiske to it. Horrified, he reminded himself he was a police officer and a man of faith.

'God will have to forgive; as for us, we'll just catch them. Let's check the jetty for a boat, McGrath.'

Hope's look told him he said the first part of that out loud. But he did not care. He was on auto-pilot, his mind struggling to deal with what he had seen. As they strode off to the jetty, back along the road, Macleod saw some of the women now being moved to different houses away from 'Fantasyland'. They were free—he needed to hold on to that.

Chapter 25

On arrival at the jetty, Macleod saw only a small tender held alongside with a single, thin outboard motor. It would have to do. Hope took a quick look for any lifejackets but they couldn't wait until they found any and so climbed into the dinghy, passing instructions to a nearby officer to contact their sergeant to coordinate further boats to the vessel just offshore.

The sea was mercifully calm and Hope sat at the fore of the boat while Macleod steered it towards the vessel before them. It was a basic but large-looking motor boat, ideal for travelling around the islands as you would appear to be another tourist. There seemed to be plenty of room below deck and no one could be seen on the vessel. There was an anchor light showing and a few lights from the port holes along the side but otherwise all seemed quiet.

Had they not seen what had happened on land? Why were they still here? Had they chosen to stay still and hope they were not seen as part of the trafficking ring? Or had she made it aboard and that was why it was all quiet?

Macleod steered the dinghy to the aft of the motorboat and Hope caught the safety wire across the vessel and then tied the dinghy onto the boat. Stepping onto the aft deck, they stayed quiet, Macleod motioning with his hands that they should enter the boat via the door before them. They could see into the first stateroom, resplendent with navy blue cushions along the sides where ornate seating was available, along with a small drinks' cabinet to one side. But everything was meticulously tidy and undisturbed. If Fiske had come aboard she had been very careful and quiet, or maybe they had all been hiding downstairs.

Stepping inside the room, Hope took the lead and pointed at the stairs that descended into the lower deck. There was no light and Macleod nodded his assent to Hope who promptly took out her penlight and started down.

From behind, Macleod watched her enter the dark and saw splashes of blood on the walls. At the foot of the short stairway, there were two choices: to proceed to the fore or the aft. Running off this corridor, which was aligned with many pictures, was a number of wooden doors and presumably cabins beyond. Macleod motioned for them to move to the aft of the boat as this was the shorter run of corridor. There were two doors this way and Hope opened the first one to find a bathroom lit up poorly by her light. It had been used but showed no untoward signs, such as the blood stains in the corridor.

Moving on to the door at the end of the corridor, Hope swung it open and then gasped at the sight before her. The room was a mess. It was meant to be a stately bedroom but cupboards were laid open and clothing had fallen down. The few chairs had been overturned and a mirror had smashed. But the most horrific sight was the man drenched in blood lying on the bed. His body was a mess and in the poor light of her small torch Hope could not make out the full extent of the body's injuries, but he must have suffered.

Macleod could see the shock on his colleague and when he stepped past her, he felt that same chill. You learnt to steel yourself when you saw such brutality as this but it still shot to your core. Walking to the corpse's head, Macleod turned it and wiped some of the blood away so he could try to identify the dead man.

'I think that's Magnus Digman,' whispered Macleod. 'Careful, she may still be on board.' With that, he stepped past Hope and started back along the main corridor. There were at least another five doors to open beyond the stairwell and Macleod took the lead this time. He stepped lightly and stood back from each door he opened. The first one was a store cupboard and had been undisturbed. The next was a small cabin with two bunks. A man lay dead in each. But these men had been killed quickly and without any extra malice, dispatched as an encumbrance, not a hated enemy.

The third door opened to another cabin but this one was empty and undisturbed. The fourth door was locked and Macleod signalled for Hope to keep a good eye on it as he opened the fifth and final door at the far end of the corridor. At first, the door hit something and then Macleod gave it a hard shove, which pushed something out of the way. He was caught by something which swung at him and then seemed to hang around his head. Adjusting the position of his penlight, he saw a pair of feet beside his head and recoiled.

Steadying himself, he passed his light over a male body, one which was brutalised and was missing some external features. It was bloody and the floor beneath it was sodden with urine and faeces as well as blood. When Macleod passed the light to the man's face, he saw an image he remembered from the photographs of the Danish soldiers. This was Oscar Borgen. He was hanging from a rope around his neck. And then the man breathed.

Macleod grabbed the feet of the man and tried to lift him up. 'Hope, help me!' But there was silence and Hope did not move to his aid.

'Step away and leave him or I'll break her neck.' The voice was calm, controlled and female. 'I mean what I say, mister policeman. And then I'll have to kill you too. But leave him to die and I'll not kill your colleague. It will be only a few more minutes. He has suffered plenty. Let it be complete.'

Macleod turned his head and saw Hope being held from behind, tightly around the throat. The pressure being exerted was causing Hope to choke and Macleod could see she was in no position to fight back. He stood looking at his colleague, his friend as she fought to breathe.

As if to help him in his deliberations about what to do, a light came on in the room and he saw the same woman who had knifed Constable Ross. There was no anger on the face, instead an almost satisfaction. As Macleod continued to push the legs of the man upward, he watched Fiske shake her head and tighten the hold on Hope's neck. There were momentary gurgles from Hope before she desperately began to struggle. Macleod thought about dropping his load and rushing forward but Fiske shook her head.

'Come closer and I'll break the neck. It will be quick, and then I'll deal with you. I am trained in these things so please do not try, mister policeman. Let go of his legs and let him die. I doubt you can save him now, but for mother's sake, I need to know for sure.'

Inside, Macleod felt himself being tossed about on the sea

of right and wrong. His integrity screaming at him to defy the woman who was running amok over the law. This was a human being he was saving, albeit an undeserving one, a poor excuse for a person and one who had committed such heinous crimes. Borgen deserved his punishment but it was not Fiske's to give. She didn't get to be the judge, jury, and executioner.

And then he saw his colleague lying dead. Hope's neck twisted to one side and her head lying at an angle that should have her screaming. But there was no sound and the ponytail lay to one side, her hair neatly lying still, as if prepared for a funeral.

God forgive me for not trying. God forgive me for judging one person above another but she is worth more than him. I will not sacrifice her life for this piece of scum. Macleod imagined every woman in the house on shore beating and hacking at Borgen with all manner of weapons. *God forgive me but there's no choice.*

And yet he knew that there was always a choice. Sometimes they are not very pleasant ones. Sometimes all the options are bad, but ultimately there is always a choice. He let go of the man's legs which dropped the few centimetres he had moved them upward. His eyes watched Fiske keeping her hold.

'You win,' spat Macleod. 'You win, he's gone.'

'Not yet he isn't,' said Fiske but the tension on Hope's neck released slightly and Macleod saw her begin to breathe easier. Her eyes opened wide and simply stared at Macleod. The feet of the man were swinging behind Macleod's back and several times they touched his shoulders as Borgen died. There were no great spasms, no final moments. The injuries sustained from Fiske's attentions had been too good, too severe. All the while, Macleod stared at Hope who looked directly back at him, eyes filled with water, either from the savageness of the choking, or from frustration at watching the man die.

After what seemed like an age, Fiske dropped her arms from Hope's throat and simply turned around, offering her hands behind her. Macleod reached for his handcuffs but they had been used back in the house.

'Cuffs, McGrath,' he ordered.

'Sir?' replied Hope, staring now at the swinging corpse.

'Your handcuffs. Secure Miss Fiske.'

It took a moment for Hope to register but then she shook her head and Macleod realised Hope had also used her own pair in the houses on shore. 'Let's move to the upper deck.' Macleod took Fiske's arm and held it up her back and he forced her, albeit as much for show as anything else, up the stairwell and to the aft of the vessel. He did not want anything on the boat sullied in case it was required for evidence. As he climbed the steps, there was a hollowness inside.

Macleod had seen people die before—it came with the job. Mostly they were dead already but he had a familiarity with death that few outside the force understood. But usually, he was engaged in trying to prevent that death, or arrived too late to stop it. Never had he had to simply stand and watch the satisfaction of a young woman, knowing her task was complete, knowing that he was powerless to uphold the law, even if the victim deserved such a death.

On the aft deck Fiske had dropped to her knees and allowed Macleod to tie her hands with rope. Given how she had operated previously, he knew she was not looking to run. In fact, he doubted that he would be alive if escape had been her plan. As Macleod stood guard over his prisoner, he saw a small boat making its way to the vessel. It was another dinghy, holding maybe three people.

'I am done, mister policeman, do not worry. I shall be no more trouble for you—it is over. You can question me and I will tell all now that my task is over. My sister is free and they have paid for what they did to my mother.'

'Do you want to see your sister?' asked Macleod. 'I don't think you got the chance. She was in the first building, nearest the main road. I managed to pull her away from a man who was . . . being entertained by her.'

'They were not in that building,' replied Fiske. 'I could not risk them escaping. They did not see me swimming out and I needed time, for they had to suffer. They made mother suffer.'

'And your sister?'

'I'm sure you will help her. You have counsellors and such things, women's refuge.'

'But do you want to see her?' asked Macleod, surprised at how distant Fiske's voice was talking about the subject.

'No, she's nothing to me. She was mother's pride, not mine.'

Ten minutes later, Macleod watched the small boat departing with Fiske now properly handcuffed and surrounded by two burly officers. But he knew she would not be an issue. There was a completeness in how she spoke, a cold and brutal end, but an end nonetheless.

Rather than take their small dinghy back to the shore, Macleod asked for officers to return in the boat and pick Hope and himself up. As they motored from earshot, Macleod looked at his colleague, and the bruising on her neck. Reaching forward, he untied her hair and let it drop before splaying it out, covering up the bruising on her neck. Hope stood without question and Macleod saw the shoulders begin to shake.

'Too close, Seoras, too bloody close.' Macleod reached forward and they embraced, clutching each other and both sniffed back tears. 'I thought you would have saved him. I thought you would have fought for him. It would have been right, would have been the right thing to do.'

'God forgive me, Hope, but you are worth a hundred of that filth below.'

'Hope stepped back. 'But every life is precious. You said that once. I thought you would always save them all, or at least try to.'

Macleod stared at her before looking her up and down. 'I used to think that too.' In the night air, he again felt a pair of feet gently tapping his shoulder as they swung into his back, time and again.

Chapter 26

'Well, what do you think?' asked Macleod.

'It's certainly a hell of a view.' Hope held a hand up to her face shielding herself from the setting sun. 'Bit hard to get to, mind, are you sure you won't need a tracker?'

Macleod stared at Hope who stuck out a tongue before sipping more of her wine. Macleod had picked out the red as it had a good name. Not being a drinker, he had no clue about which wine was which, only that the bottles seemed to vary greatly in price. But Jane had told him what to buy and she had already helped herself to half the bottle before disappearing into their new house to attend to some undisclosed manner. In other words, she is giving us some space, thought Macleod.

'You didn't have to invite me out here, much as the food and company is appreciated,' said Hope. 'I'm doing fine.'

'Who said it was for you?' laughed Macleod. 'You weren't the only one who got spooked that night.'

'I hardly think spooked covers it.'

'Do you still get the dreams?' asked Macleod.

'Vividly.' Hope had not turned around to answer but was still staring out at the firth before her.

'Can't be easy waking to that, alone.' The last word had

arrived just a little too late and the emphasis sat on it rather that statement before.

'Are you fishing?' asked Hope.

'For what?'

'The state of my love life.'

'No,' said Macleod, a little too quickly. 'I'm just concerned. Glasgow can be a lonely place to wake up in, even if there are so many people around you. I did that for years.'

'Who said I was waking up in Glasgow?'

Macleod let the comment go and walked over to Hope, standing beside her and looking at the sea too. 'It's in the middle of the night, a touch on my shoulder, a tap, followed by another and if I turn around, there's a pair of feet swinging.'

'I thought you would have seen enough to not be bothered by that sort of thing,' said Hope.

'The day it doesn't bother you, I think you lose something. Even the whole setup they had at the houses, it still chills me, what those poor women would go through, all for sport, for entertainment.' Macleod placed his hand on Hope's shoulder. 'But I wouldn't change my mind, I still say you are worth more than him any day.'

'My neck's not quite right yet,' said Hope, trying to change the tone. 'Whatever she did exactly, the muscles are not right. Still sore to twist it.'

'I'll see you at the trial, won't I?' said Macleod. 'It's going to be strange, working with someone else again.'

Hope nodded. 'Yeah, I'll be there. Though I doubt it'll last long, what with Fiske's confession to it all. It was Malthe Amundsen I felt sorry for. After Anna Fiske was destroyed by those men from his troop, he basically helped Anna in every way; it wasn't his fault that the life of her daughter went sour.

After all, he found her a loving family by adoption, after he got Anna the job over here.'

'Life doesn't always work out,' said Macleod. 'What happened with her daughter going into foster care and eventually leaving before getting taken into that ring, that was just tragic. And then Amundsen helping to find her. But the anger never died and she passed that onto her second daughter. Freja Fiske had no chance, burdened by her mother's hate—that was all she had. When we freed her sister, she didn't even ask to see her, she didn't care. All she wanted was to satisfy her now dead mother. I feel for her; she had a burden that she never should have had. And she'll never lose it.'

'Guess a bad neck was not such a bad result after all.' Hope walked over to a small box container and looked at some newly planted flowers. 'I didn't know you liked plants.'

'Not me, Jane. She's got me running back and forward to the garden centre in Inverness like they're going to sell out. She's got an eye for it though, not like me. I had to replant that section by the wall because I put in the wrong blasted colours as she put it.'

'So, you've bought the house, moved up north, and what now? Are you going to make a decent woman of her?'

'The hell he is,' laughed Jane as she re-emerged from the house. 'I told him, I did marriage before and the guy was an arse. More than that actually, but Seoras doesn't like me to swear. So, I warned him, this is a day-by-day promise, so he'd better stay on his toes.'

Hope smirked and caught Macleod's eye. 'Don't encourage her,' said Macleod.

'Was he telling you, he's waking me up in the night, claiming he's had a fright? I mean, I understand the code and I'm there with my womanly charms to satisfy his wanton needs.'

'You are outrageous,' shrieked Macleod before laughing.

'But he's doing well, aren't you Seoras. My man's doing well.' Jane ran a hand onto Macleod's neck and he felt somewhat uncomfortable with this open show of love in front of Hope. But he knew with Jane he had better get used to it.

'Anyway,' continued Jane, 'when's your man showing up?'

Hope shook her head at Jane as Macleod looked on in surprise. 'What man?' he asked.

'You didn't tell him?'

'No,' replied Hope, 'not yet. But I think I hear a car outside.'

Macleod watched Hope disappear around the side of his house and Jane wrapped her arms around him. 'A man, she didn't say.'

'Some detective you are,' teased Jane.

'I thought she might have said.'

'Don't be annoyed, it's because of you two, how you are.'

'What do you mean? She's just my colleague,' said Macleod.

'No, she's not. She's a bit more than that to you. You're fond of her, as a person, and she reaches your other side too, you know which side I mean.' Macleod looked down at his feet, almost ashamed. 'That's fine, she's a heck of a good-looking woman, Seoras. And you got close with work, and all the stuff about your wife. But I know who you want to be with. If you didn't, I wouldn't be here. You're lucky to find colleagues like that.'

Macleod wrapped his arms around Jane and kissed her like no one was watching.

'Sorry to barge in.'

Macleod tried to release Jane but she was not having any of it and it was another five seconds before he was able to recover and see who Hope had arrived back with. As Jane laughed at being caught in a moment, Macleod looked with surprise at the Sergeant he knew so well standing beside Hope.

'Allinson, good to see you again.' Macleod said the words like they were the most natural thing in the world but his face betrayed him as he looked on in shock at Hope's arm wrapped around the man's waist. 'Very happy for you both, but the distance has got to be a thing.'

Macleod felt a nudge in his ribs and Jane looked up at him. 'Let alone what's not yours to ask about.'

Hope laughed at Macleod's scolded face. 'You're not the only one who can move.'

'Where you going?' asked Macleod and he saw Allinson smile.

'I thought my man was doing enough running to Glasgow, so I'm going to come up here. I've applied for a transfer and I reckon the new boss might be a soft touch.'

'I've been out of the office for three weeks,' said Macleod with his jaw dropping open. He felt like he was the only person not aware of a joke but at least it was a pleasant one.

Later that evening, Macleod was standing again watching the firth and in particular a small cargo vessel which was slowly making its way out to sea. There was little motion on board and Macleod wondered what it must be like to stand on that bridge just letting the hours while away as the blue disappeared behind you.

'It is a great view.' Hope stood beside Macleod and smiled at him. 'You've done well with Jane. I always thought she was good fun for you but she's a lot more than that. I'm delighted for you, both of you.'

'She is something else. But what about you? Is he your Jane?'

Hope burst out laughing. 'Not even going to try and point out how wrong that analogy is. No, he's not, Seoras. Not yet anyway. But he's a good man and a real comfort. He's moving aside, changing to another department to let me come up. Said we shouldn't work together; it would compromise him if I was in danger. He's probably right.'

'Of course. You can't work with someone you love, not with the dangers we face. It's hard enough with colleagues you're very fond of.'

'Yes, it is, Seoras. It wasn't just you who was very fond of me. Just happy to see you're happy.'

'Good. It's all good then.'

Hope touched his shoulder. 'I think it is.'

'Good. So, when are you becoming a Detective Sergeant then?'

Turn over to discover the new Patrick Smythe series!

Start your Patrick Smythe journey here!

Patrick Smythe is a former Northern Irish policeman who after suffering an amputation after a bomb blast, takes to the sea between the west coast of Scotland and his homeland to ply his trade as a private investigator. Join Paddy as he tries to work to his own ethics while knowing how to bend the rules he once enforced. Working from his beloved motor boat 'Craigantlet', Paddy decides to rescue a drug mule in this short story from the pen of G R Jordan.

Join G R Jordan's monthly newsletter about forthcoming releases and special writings for his tribe of avid readers and then receive your free Patrick Smythe short story.

Goto https://bit.ly/PatrickSmythe for your Patrick Smythe journey to start!

About the Author

GR Jordan is a self-published author who finally decided at forty that in order to have an enjoyable lifestyle, his creative beast within would have to be unleashed. His books mirror that conflict in life where acts of decency contend with self-promotion, goodness stares in horror at evil, and kindness blindsides us when we at our worst. Corrupting our world with his parade of wondrous and horrific characters, he highlights everyday tensions with fresh eyes whilst taking his methodical, intelligent mainstays on a roller-coaster ride of dilemmas, all the while suffering the banter of their provocative sidekicks.

A graduate of Loughborough University where he masqueraded as a chemical engineer but ultimately played American football, Gary had worked at changing the shape of cereal flakes and pulled a pallet truck for a living. Watching vegetables freeze at -40'C was another career highlight and he was also one of the Scottish Highlands "blind" air traffic controllers.

These days he has graduated to answering a telephone to people in trouble before telephoning other people to sort it out.

Having flirted with most places in the UK, he is now based in the Isle of Lewis in Scotland where his free time is spent between raising a young family with his wife, writing, figuring out how to work a loom and caring for a small flock of chickens. Luckily, his writing is influenced by his varied work and life experience as the chickens have not been the poetical inspiration he had hoped for!

You can connect with me on:
- ⊕ https://grjordan.com
- 🐦 https://twitter.com/carpetless
- 🅕 https://facebook.com/carpetlessleprechaun

Subscribe to my newsletter:
- ✉ https://bit.ly/PatrickSmythe

Also by G R Jordan

G R Jordan writes across multiple genres including crime, dark and action adventure fantasy, feel good fantasy, mystery thriller and horror fantasy. Below are a selection of his work grouped together in their genres. Whilst all books are available across online stores, signed copies are available at his personal shop.

Dead at Third Man: A Highlands and Islands Detective Thriller (Highlands & Islands Detective Book 5)
A landmark cricket club is formed in the heart of the Western Isles. A gala opening leaves a battered body in the changing room when stumps is called. Can Macleod and McGrath find the killer before the rest of the team are bowled out?

In the fifth outing of this tenacious pair, Macleod and McGrath return to the Isle of Lewis when the first match of the newly formed cricket club ends in murder. Uncovering the tensions in the fledgling organisation, they must sort sporting angst from deadly intent if they are to uncover the true reason for the formation of this strange enterprise. Can they discover what bloody crimes sully the perfect whites of the starting XI?

Don't step beyond your crease or you might just be stumped!

 **The Disappearance of Russell Hadleigh: A Patrick Smythe Mystery Thriller #1** A retired judge fails to meet his golf partner. His wife calls for help while running a fantasy play ring. When Russians start co-opting into a fairly-traded clothing brand, can Paddy untangle the strands before the bodies start littering the golf course?

In his first full novel, Patrick Smythe, the single-armed former policeman, must infiltrate the golfing social scene to discover the fate of his client's husband. Assisted by a young starlet of the greens, Paddy tries to understand just who bears a grudge and who likes to play in the rough, culminating in a high stakes showdown where lives are hanging by the reaction of a moment. If you love pacey action, suspicious motives and devious characters, then Paddy Smythe operates amongst your kind of people.

Love is a matter of taste but money always demands more of its suitor.

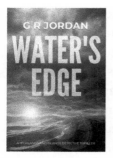

Water's Edge: A Highlands and Islands Detective Thriller (Highlands & Islands Detective Book 1)
https://grjordan.com/product/waters-edge

A body discovered by the rocks. A broken detective returns to a scene of past tragedy. Will the pain of the past prevent him from seeing the present?

Detective Inspector Macleod returns to his island home twenty years after the painful loss of his wife. With a disposition forged in strong religious conservatism, he must bond with his new partner, the free spirited and upcoming female star of the force, to seek the killer of a young woman and shine a light on the evil beneath the surface. To do so, he must once again stand in the place where he lost everything. Only at the water's edge, will everything be made new.

The rising tide brings all things to the surface.

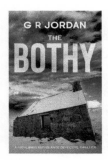

The Bothy: A Highlands and Islands Detective Thriller (Highlands & Islands Detective Book 2)
https://grjordan.com/product/the-bothy
Two bodies in a burnt out love nest. A cultish lifestyle and children moulded by domination. Can Macleod unravel the Black Isle mystery before the killer dispenses judgement again?

DI Macleod heads for the Black Isle as winter sets in to unravel the mystery of two lovers in a burned out bothy. With his feisty partner DC McGrath, he must unravel the connection between a family living under a cultish cloud and a radio station whose staff are being permanently retired. In the dark of winter, can Macleod shine a light on the shadowy relationships driving a killer to their murderous tasks?

Forgetting your boundaries has never been so deadly!

The Horror Weekend (Highlands & Islands Detective Book 3)

https://grjordan.com/product/the-horror-weekend

A last-minute replacement on a role-playing weekend. One fatal accident after another. Can Macleod overcome the snowstorm from hell to stop a killer before the guest list becomes obsolete?

Detectives Macleod and McGrath join a bizarre cast of characters at a remote country estate on the Isle of Harris where fantasy and horror are the order of the day. But when regular accidents happen, Macleod sees a killer at work and needs to uncover what links the dead. Hampered by a snowstorm that has closed off the outside world, he must rely on Hope McGrath before they become one of the victims.

It's all a game…, but for whom?

9 781912 153633